A Traveller Came By

STORIES ABOUT DYING

to the memory of
LORNA McINNIS SMITHIES
gay and unvanquished spirit

A TRAVELLER CAME BY

STORIES ABOUT DYING

SEÁN VIRGO

THISTLEDOWN PRESS

Canadian Cataloguing in Publication Data
Virgo, Seán, 1940–

A traveller came by : stories about dying
ISBN 1-894345-19-3
1. Death—Fiction.   I. Title.
PS8593.I72 T73 2000   C813'.54   C00-920204-8
PR9199.3.V56 T73 2000

Cover photograph "Islanders of Inisheer", 1898 by J.M. Synge
(Every effort has been made to obtain permission to use the cover photograph)
Typeset by Thistledown Press Ltd.
Printed and bound in Canada

Thistledown Press Ltd.
633 Main Street
Saskatoon, Saskatchewan S7H 0J8
Canada
www.thistledown.sk.ca

Thistledown Press gratefully acknowledges the financial assistance of the
Canada Council for the Arts, the Saskatchewan Arts Board, and the
Government of Canada through the Book Publishing Industry Development
Program for its publishing program.

A TRAVELLER CAME BY

Whan I thenke thynges three
Ne may I nevere blithe be:
That oon is that I shal awey;
That other is I ne wot which day;
The thridde is my moste care —
I ne wot whider I shall fare.
[Anonymous — 13th Century]

INTRODUCTION

There is a small farmhouse on the north shore of Lesbos, with two rooms and a kitchen, and verandas along its north and east walls. It looks out, from a shallow bay, across the Turkish straits to Anatolia. Each day the wind blows through, from the West, tempering the dry heat of summer and keeping the fierce *kounupio* flies at bay. For six months in 1986, I spent my days on the north veranda, at a crude, low table, where by mid-afternoon the clacking of my little manual typewriter played counterpoint to the whirligig flutter of manuscript sheets by my feet. Pinned down to the cement floor by a rough beach stone, my unfinished novel never ceased struggling to escape, fly off and scatter itself upon the sea wind.

That stone is in front of me now, on my desk: a paperweight still, though with no Aegean breeze to resist. The stone has a life, for me, and a memory — a series of memories — though in the lifespan of a stone the memories of one man can only lie skin deep.

The sea wind of Lesbos fails just at sunset. Then the island itself breathes out for an hour, sighing the day's warmth back through the straits, before it lies still. The verandas filled up with perfume, the soft air distilled from the night-scented stocks and nicotianas that the owners had planted below the grapevines.

Then nighttime's enchantments took over. The nightingales sang unceasingly in the thickets, two fields away, where a stream ran out onto the beach; and the frogs cried, as they had in Aristophanes' time, *koaxx-axx-axx-axx-axx*. The many-toned sheepbells of the flocks in the olive groves carried down to the house in waves of sound, as though a cascade of blending waters were waking, and falling asleep, and spilling again out of the low hills towards us. When Selene, the Greek moon, was dark, the great constellation of Kiknos, the Swan, soared over those hills and the highlands beyond them.

These things are still there, of course, as they have been for centuries, enduring in the actual world as they do in my memory.

The setting is, to say the least, idyllic. There are just four houses above the curving beach, three of them owned by Athenians and empty except for two weeks every August. Around the farmhouse is a garden half-acre, which the owners come out from the village to work in each day: watering and picking their way through the wide rows of tomatoes, zuchinis, eggplants, watermelons, okra. The handle of the well-pump still screeches and moans, I am sure, and summons a love-lorn response from the old jackass across the stream, crying the same seesaw *hee-haw* that D.H.Lawrence heard in Sicily seventy years back: "All mares are dead, All mares are dead, I can't bear it!"

Along the stone walls are fig trees and lemons, and behind is a small olive orchard, beyond which the hills climb to the south, alive with springs as on no other Greek island, and dark with olive groves. The garden gate opens straight onto the bay. The coarse sand of the beach is sleeked by the narrow Aegean tides and by midday becomes almost too hot to walk on. Dolphins play out at the point each afternoon, the sea is that ink-blue of childhood, and the water is so dense and warm that you can lie in it, rocked by the groundswell as if in a hammock, and stare up at the Greek sky or the stars.

"I am a child of Earth, and of starry Heaven," sang Orpheus, first maker of poetry and music: "*Geis pais eimi, kai ouranou asteroentos . . .* " His music charmed the wild things and the winds, and the gateway of Death opened, spellbound, to his song, so that he walked with the dead and came near to bringing life back to Eurydice, his beloved. " . . . *autar emoi genos ouranion*" — "but my Race is of Heaven alone." When he was murdered, the Aegean waves carried his head, still singing, to the shores of Lesbos.

It is the sort of place writers, and would-be writers, dream of. But one of the ironies of a writer's life is that the perfect time, the perfect place, so often prove sterile: you spend your days in the planned-for, saved-for retreat, reading the thrillers left behind by a previous tenant, or entertaining garrulous local characters, or simply exploring the landscape. Then you tell yourself this has happened before, and that nothing is wasted; that the work's going on unconsciously, and that when you get home you'll find time, somehow, for it there. There is something truly perverse about that pattern, but the farmhouse at Kaiya broke it for me.

I had come to Greece, in April that year, on the instinct that I would find a place, and a seclusion, that would allow me to finish the book I'd been grappling with for almost six years. Well, the angels, as they say, were on my side.

That farmhouse was a gift from beyond the grave. I was able to afford the time, and the primitive luxury of the place, because my father had played his own secret game with the angels.

When he'd died, two years before, my sister and I had discovered three bankbooks — one in the table beside his easy chair, the others in his bureau — in separate drawers, untouched, and perhaps forgotten, for several years. There were also, here and there in the old house, various sheets of legal-sized paper, covered with lines and columns of two- and three-digit numbers.

It was my sister's children who broke part of the code, and dug out another bankbook from the secret bureau drawer only they knew about. My mother, in her wheel-chair, was roused from her dazed bereavement more than once to laugh at the zany treasure-hunt. My father — a teetotaller who hid his shyness and deep privacy behind an unfailing jollity and a trick of asking endless, intelli-gent questions to avoid real conversation — had been bet-ting on horses, with some inscrutable system of his own devising (that part of the code went unbroken with him to the grave). He had not grown rich — the forgotten bankbooks prove that was not the point — but he'd won far more than he'd lost.

My mother, who was so involved in their life together that she died, as her doctor told us she would, within a year, had no idea that her husband was a gambling man. After her death, there was some money for me that was never expected — a joke and a secret from beyond the grave. Did he feel that I spent it well, on my own kind of gamble? (I certainly don't have his flair for the horses. On the morning of his funeral, I thought we should lay a bet for him and found a horse in the fifth race at Kildare called Poppy's Girl — we called him "Pop" — at long odds. I bet a fiver to win, and the horse came in second. Another laugh from the hereafter — or a warning, maybe!)

An owl and a Cherokee girl led me to the farmhouse on Kaiya strand (but that is another story), and I was blessed almost at once with the compulsion to write, sitting all day on the vine-wreathed veranda, taking breaks every two or three hours to swim in the bay or climb up through the olive groves, but wandering, in truth, not in Greece but in the quite different landscape of my novel. There was almost nothing to distract me.

The nearest village was two miles away, and except on three public holidays the beach was virtually deserted until August. A straggle of shepherds came through in the lambing weeks, the occasional farmer went up to divert a stream and irrigate his orchards, and Àthena and Manòli, my landlords, were there each morning, cheerful and unobtrusive, murmuring or singing in the garden. The few foreign visitors to the beach bore the "traveller not tourist" stamp — people who'd come for the place, not the action. There was no action.

So my work progressed, and I knew I would finish my novel. Sometimes it felt as though it were writing me. The sheep bells and nightingales and frogs, the cicadas in the fig trees, the lovesick jackass yearning for the well-pump, the whistle and whirr of the foraging turtle doves' wings — those, with the dry, braiding scents of oregano, marjoram, lemon-flowers and ripening figs, formed the texture of my days, and are the texture of my memories. Perhaps the other old genii of Lesbos, the 6th-century BC poets, Alcaeus and Sappho, were there in spirit; perhaps, with Orpheus, they'd breathed into the landscape a fondness for writers; who can say? (There were darker ghosts, too — they made off with my Cherokee girl, though that's also another story.)

One day I came out of that royal-blue water, in late afternoon, and met Asher and Katie Fortuin. I guess, after two months, I was ready for company; maybe our meeting was intended — in any case, I did not resent them upon "my" beach. We started talking. From Amsterdam, they were serious, light-hearted people, graceful in mind and body, courteous, original, and with that European aptitude for languages which makes most of us feel like barbarians. They came in for coffee, and immediately, without fear of intrusion on either side, we became friends.

Asher is a doctor, a specialist in palliative care, a friend and healer of the dying. It did not surprise me to think that the dying could be healed (as opposed to being cured) but Asher made this, the most "hopeless" branch of medicine, seem the most vital. When he began to speak about his work, my veranda fell under a different kind of spell. I don't know that I've ever met anyone who had so completely married "his avocation to his vocation." He was, I could feel it, a happy man. We three took turns in speaking of ourselves, but it is his lean hands' eloquence that I remember, shaping the essence of his words as the daylight faded in the garden. His mission in life was a continuum: there will always be death; the goal of a healer like Asher is achieved every working day.

I realized very soon that one of the foreign tongues he had set out to master was the language of death, the baffling yet simple dialect, with its challenging quirks of humour, that is heard in the foothills and marches of Hamlet's "undiscovered country from whose bourne No traveller returns."

Here was no burned-out, dispirited technician, in flight from the treadmill; the Fortuins shared a sort of calm enthusiasm, a childlike alertness to what Lesbos might offer the mind and the senses. They watched, and listened; and there were long moments, as the fragrant dusk closed around us, of complete, grateful silence, with Asher and myself leaning back against the house wall, and Katie in lovely, almost yogic repose at the veranda's edge, her features lifted to the moonglow behind the hills, as the first stars woke over the bay.

The moon was just past the full; when it broke free of the ridge it lit their way home to the village. I watched from my gate as they went back along the beach, hand in hand, and their figures merged into the tamarisk shadows where the village path turned inland. The bay was very still, just the faint hushing of the tide creeping in. Some nights the *soupia* boats would come round to Kaiya, and their naptha lamps would pop into life and hiss, incandescent and spectral, above the water; but that night there was nothing, and I followed my slanting moonshadow down to the sea's edge and stood there in that mood, akin to first love, which follows the meeting of minds, the glancing of destinies.

Across the straits there was a pulse and stab of light, and then darkness again. Small wonder that Matthew Arnold's lines, "On the French coast the light Gleams and is gone" unfurled in my mind. Worlds do connect, across cultures and across time, just as Arnold's thoughts had moved out from the cliffs of Dover to Sophocles on the Aegean, where I stood now, and had heard, as I now imagined I heard, "the eternal note of sadness". What else can we feel, alone with time and the elements? It is Wordsworth's "still, sad music of humanity". But that sadness is a commonality, and holds its own consolation.

Of course, Asher had asked to read my work; I had lent him a copy of my first book of stories, *White Lies & Other Fictions*, to take back to the village. When he and Katie came over to Kaiya, a couple of days later, he had read the whole book, and wanted to talk. He was, as non-literary people can be, almost the perfect reader. He had not only read my stories, and wanted to *show* that he'd read them, he had actually entered the worlds I'd constructed, and treated my "characters" as real, as intimates, as friends.

But his enthusiasm for one story, "Death Bed", dominated. He had made it his own. He must have copies of it, he said; he would use it. Stories, stories like this one, were what the dying had most need of in the modern world — most need, and most lack.

Asher's father was Jewish, and had survived the Nazi occupation of Holland through a mixture of luck, the help of friends, German stupidity, and a kind of shapeshifting effrontery. Perhaps the Hasidic devotion to story — the belief that stories lead to understanding, even to survival, and reflect the Creation at its most simple and mysterious — formed part of his son's inheritance. But it was a strange thought, for me, that something I had written — an attempt to enter the minds of two old men, from two cultures different to my own, on the threshold of death — might make sense, and give consolation or guidance to someone dying of cancer in an Amsterdam hospice.

Stories about death may console, by giving a shape to or making sense of things, but Asher Fortuin wanted stories where dying was not suffered or endured, or simply, obscurely, happened. Stories about power and alertness. To die, he believed, is to do something, to go somewhere, to leave rather than to be left. "We should be able to say 'my death', he told me, "at least as accurately as we say 'my life'."

But one does not write fiction for a particular audience, or with particular theories to illustrate. Quite simply, one sets out to create life. So I was disconcerted by Asher's view of my work. I was glad he believed in that story, and touched that it might be useful to him in his practice, but I knew I could never set out to write anything with a "medical" function in mind.

I have, though, continued to write about dying, and death. I don't know why — I'm in no way a morbid person, and the stories have always been about people, not victims, as far as I'm concerned, and quite often tinged by laughter. And you can't ask an artist — you can't ask yourself — why certain subjects keep demanding your attention. The artist who can answer that question is no longer an artist. In any case, the stories I've written about dying have been widely spaced, with their places in various collections, and I would never have thought that they might belong together, in their own book.

Except that, as time has passed, the Grey Death of Cancer, the White Death of AIDS have taken their toll of my friends, and I've kept vigil by hospital beds and cursed our culture for its ignorance. By making Death our final taboo, we have thrust it out of our reach.

We may, as Yeats says in his wonderful incantation, have "created Death", but when he claims that we "know Death to the bone" he is surely whistling in the wind.

It was when I sat at one of those bedsides, in the well-intentioned wasteland of a modern hospital, that I found myself, with absolutely no entitlement other than instinct, giving a friend advice and directions on his journey. (I'll describe this moment in my preface to the story, "Guardians".) I had no entitlement, perhaps, but I *felt* entitled. I remembered the photograph of a dying Gypsy chieftain and his heir, holding the same wooden chair as the spirit passed over, each giving to each. I gave my friend the bones of a story, a sketch of the map he would need.

To put it a better way, I told him a bedtime story. Or, rather, I started one. It would be his to finish. I've no doubt that he did. (And maybe sometime, in a dream, he will tell me how that story really ends.)

There's another way, maybe, to look at what we shared in that Winnipeg hospital room, in defiance of the catheters, monitors, tubes. When my daughters were young, I would finish my bedtime stories by wishing them the "best dreams in the world". I hoped — believed even — that I had left John with that blessing at least, as he slipped towards the Big Sleep, if sleep is what it is. I was just a voice, after all, on the borders of that dreaming, but hearing, they say, is the last sense to fail. And as all who read or tell stories, especially to children, know: if you see and believe, if you hear and touch and smell the world of your story, the listeners will hear and enter it, too.

We are no lonelier in death, I imagine, than in life. People take such pains, such drugs and such distractions to avoid loneliness, yet most of our richest experiences come when we are alone. Or so I have found. We are never alone, of course, in the Creation, the natural world, the Universe — call that wide, turbulent harmony what you will — but we so often must feel alone, or have solitude thrust upon us, even to pay attention to the Creation.

I have spent time in places where death is neither a terror nor a taboo. I envy those cultures for what we have lost, for our forebears all had it once. A Bauro man explained to me once in Makira, with the tender forebearance of a teacher who is stating the obvious, that the Uncle he dreamed of last night was both dead and alive: "We ate together, we went to the shore, he gave me advice." In the same village, a five year old boy was called "*Tatai*" — "Grandfather" — by all his family: he could still act like a child, but when there was need he took on the authority of the old man reborn in him. There are people, too, on our own west coast who understand, casually, the nature of reincarnation, and watch with delight the traits of the dead in their children. Such is the Haida *hoonts*, the fourfold rebirth.

Each culture has its own truths and realities, but in all those places, dying and mourning are intimately ritualized and experienced. The Haida family in the story "Death Bed", which my Dutch friend so valued, are struggling to preserve that reality in the face of European customs. My own grandparents would have been horrified at the idea of dying in a hospital.

Asher Fortuin's distinction between healing and curing has other bearings on our culture. It seems to me that a faith in medical science is the overwhelming superstition of our age, even for those who still have religious convictions. A cure for almost anything is bound to turn up. So modern specialists, whose efforts are aimed at a cure, take on the unnatural role of oracle and elder for many of their patients. But so few specialists are healers: quite apart from the pressures and stresses of their jobs, their expertise is of the flesh, not the spirit, and they are unequipped, unfit in fact, and too often disinclined, to give what is really needed.

I know of no loneliness greater, no more terrible pathos — with the horror that it conceals — than a person's dying with his or her last, imploring hopes fixed on the machines of modern technology and the mechanics who operate them, or on the drugs whose workings are an irrevocable mystery to the life that is ending.

Dying people are vitally concerned with life, if they're allowed. They are not lepers, or saints, or objects. And if they need stories about Death, too, as Asher Fortuin insisted to me, it must be because the folklore of Death has withered — gone down in the twentieth century with so many other dialects. Even humour, mankind's dance with taboo, has failed in this area for most of us. And with that dialect has been lost the sense of relationship with the dead that I've envied in older cultures.

We need that relationship; we are literally lost without it. It may be with family, forebears or friends; it may be with the intimate voices of Mozart, or Emily Dickinson, or Pablo Picasso (as in Paul McCartney's lovely elegy: "Drink to me, Drink to my health, You know I can't drink any more . . . "). D'Arcy McGee, for whom life seemed a far deeper mystery than death, wrote this prayer for a young friend: "Thus would I have him school, in humbleness, His ear to catch the rhythmic admonitions Which come, upon the wings of every wind, From the far shore where the dead ages dwell." Even if you don't see the dead as "piling up on the other side" you eventually realize that far more of the people who would claim kinship with you, and care for you, are there (whether or not they are waiting and watching) than here. Why should this be a lonely discovery?

I learned and translated a *Lost At Night* song, or chant, from one of the West Coast native cultures. It has an upbeat rhythm that mocks its own terror, but it deals with terror all the same: of the known, the unknown, the half-known; and its consolation lies simply in the fact that the song has been sung before, for generations, against the same perils and terrors — that as you sing it you are in company with your grandfather, and with his grandfather, all lost in the forest together; and that your song of distress calls and draws you back into your family, as though round the hearth, shielded and held from the phantoms of despair. (My invocation of Matthew Arnold, like his of Sophocles, on that Aegean strand, was a version of this.)

Even the consolations of religion, without a supporting culture, have the colour of loneliness: they embrace death, at least, by rejecting or relegating life in favour of the hereafter. They require more than faith, they demand obedience; and though that, in our weakest moments, may seem like a consolation, it exiles the human spirit that still wishes to explore, not just submit. I am not attacking religion; I know myself as religious. When a religion and the culture it shapes are at one (which means that it informs our day-to-day *life*) then it deals in effective truth because it reaffirms (rather than abnegates) the human spirit and its place in the transhuman family. It defines continuity.

Fear and Grief are the root and weather of dying, and I don't want to seem to downplay them, nor the dread which shrouds the unknown country, nor the often convulsive sense of loss, or heartbreak, which besets the dying and those they are leaving. (Again, I say "leaving", not "taken from", because I'm talking of those for whom dying is a conscious process. Infants — if they are not, in fact, still angels — and the victims of accidents, crimes and seizures, are indeed "taken," but our culture still has prescriptions for the bereaved, for "getting on with life.")

But one folklore of death, at least, survives in our culture. It goes, "If you were given six months to live, how would you spend it?" (Notice, even here, the "given" which places the doctor in God's place.) Underlying the question — which is a game for the living to play, of course — is the absolute, unconditional sentence of death. There's no hope, and from that supposedly hopeless position unfolds the whole positive, life-relishing repertoire of the answers: the visit to Machu Picchu, the rollicking through bawdy houses, the canoe trip into the Arctic, the week at the Louvre — whatever it may be. And isn't that strange? You offer a healthy man or woman a death sentence and they choose life at its most intense; tell someone they're really dying, and nine times out of ten they start to shut down, put on the leper's hood, or prepare — though the odds may be hundreds to one — to have their cells "nuked" or poisoned. Simply clinging to breath (and especially trusting in others to cling to it for you) is not being alive. Pain can be dealt with; the poppy retains its ancient power. And there is life still to be discovered.

Some will think me defeatist, though. There are those who can, with cold eyes, grab medicine by the scruff of its neck and *use it*. They have their own future imperatives. But these stories are for the dying: those who literally live with death. By all means "rage against the dying of the light", if that is not someone else's demand and so long as the rage is not, in fact, blind.

We prepare best for death, surely, by loving life. Rather than a death's head *memento mori* over my desk, I'd choose Walter De la Mare's bittersweet prescription: "Look thy last on all things lovely, every hour . . . " It's much more than a "Gather ye rosebuds" hedonism: the sense of mortality in it is life's enrichment.

No one experiences mortality — or love, or ecstasy, or beauty — so intensely and personally as the conventionally "immune and invulnerable" adolescent. There's an adolescence in all celebration of life. The dying, whether old or young, can be wonderfully "immature".

They're intensely symbolic, too. Dying is a poetic state of being, because it reaches for luminous images. These may be very homely, or quite extravagant, but they are layered with meaning and purpose, like the cherished lines in a poem, the gesture in a painting, the cadence in a sonata, the half-door in a dream: distillations of the world, or of memory, that you can hold as your own. In a small way the stone from Kaiya that sits on my desk, that I'm picking up now, as I write (no, I'm not a one-handed typist — I write my first drafts in ink) is just such an image.

I did not choose it as a touchstone (though it may have chosen me); I'd just needed a paperweight. But it held down my novel, was touched by me every day in that period of Grace, and was the last thing I packed before I walked along Kaiya, and turned up the path to the village, for the last time. It's grey, with a faint flush of rose to it sometimes, its rougher parts almost black, with here and there, when I turn it in the light, the wink of mica. It's heart shaped, I guess — like the actual, lop-shouldered organ, not the Valentine emblem — and it's strangely heavy for its size.

It is dense, as I've said, with meaning for me: associations, memories, loss and delight. It's my father's legacy. It's Orpheus' song. It's the words of that novel. It's the Cherokee girl. It's who I have been. And it's Kaiya.

It has its own life, too, as a stone: a future, as well as a past, beyond mine. Human memories, indeed, can lie only skin deep. Even when an epitaph is carved into stone, and even in the eternal climate of Greece, the letters fade and anyway say no more than "someone was here". But what more should we want?

If I have choice, it will be one of the treasures that have found me over the years which I will have close by when I'm dying — to linger upon with my eyes, to touch a last time with the hand that, I suppose, will be becoming a stranger's . . .

I have chosen eleven stories for this bedside book. Five have never been published, the rest come from four collections, published over the last fifteen years. None of them was written with this book, or purpose, in mind.

Stories, fictions, are made to be explored and experienced, not explained. And I would be the last to interpret what I've written. But I've prefaced each story with a brief explanation of how and when it came to be written; and sometimes I've said (without at all insisting that I am right) what I find in it.

I don't know — it may seem presumptuous to speak and write about dying and, in some of the stories, about what follows after. I have only my imagination to guide me. Yet we live only through the play of the imagination.

And if some of these stories are alive, as I hope they may be, then for most of their readers they'll be gifts from beyond the grave. And surely by then, I'll seem entitled.

I would wish myself, and you, the "best dreams in the world".

Or out of it.

prelude

Twenty-five years after I wrote this story I still sometimes read it in public. It makes people laugh.

If we can laugh over death by cancer, using humour to face it rather than to wish it away, I think we've achieved something. We've humanised the unthinkable.

The story is set 50 years ago, in a small rural world, and much has changed, superficially at least, in that time. But I think people in Québec, in France, in Italy, in Greece — in any "priest-ridden" society — could still relate to a world that is both superstitious and deeply anti-clerical; where the puritan, restrictive morality preached by the churches is largely supported by the women, while the men acknowledge the Rabelaisian foibles of the "Old Adam".

Val Goram in this story is neither a kind nor a good man, but the people need his defiant courage as a touchstone, as they need examples of saintliness, cowardice, avarice and excess. Every society creates a kind of theatre out of itself — a full cast of extreme characters to remind people who they are. Without that theatre, and the humour it unleashes, a society suffocates. (The criminal underworld and the corrupt bureaucrats in Soviet Russia were — unconsciously of course — heroes of human nature against the puritan myths of the regime.)

Val Goram's last act is played out for an audience which includes two young boys. They see mischief at work, more potent than death. Val's defiance of everything hypocritical cuts the adult tribe down to size. "Ain't death a grand thing," say Mourteen as they scamper away. Well it ain't, really, but that's a better way than most for a child to start learning mortality.

This may be the only outright comedy in this collection, but most of the stories have at least flashes and stabs of laughter in them. I don't know if it's a peculiarly "Irish" trait to laugh at death (it's not at all the same as Scottish "gallows humour"), but there's certainly a strong tradition there. "Death?" said Brendan Behan. "Sure it's the last thing on earth I'd be thinking about." And when he was actually dying: "God bless you, sister," to a nun in attendance. "May you have a son grow up to be a bishop."

I originally wrote "Shan Val Mór" to exorcise the same rage of betrayal that the "old sinner" still clings to. I'm glad to see that I kept my sense of humour even in that situation, and the irony is that my angers don't have the staying power that old Val's did. One of my "betrayers" is the closest of friends to this day; and when the other — a wise, droll, wonderfully gifted man — died last year, too young, too young, I felt the world's loss as deeply as anyone could have.

SHAN VAL MÓR

We were ditching in the lake field when Peadar Cullin called down that Shan Val Mór was brought home from the hospital and was for dying immediately.

"Has he the Father to him?" my father shouted.

"They say evening will be time enough," said Peader and whipped off in his ass cart.

"Divil a priest he'll want by if he's in his senses," said my granda. He put by his spade and reached for his pipe.

Granda always seemed the lazy one, though he'd worked hard, man and boy, for sixty some years. It was the easy way about him though, and his smoking and chat. I was proud of my granda: they all said he was a gas man and there'd be grand craic wherever he went calling. At seventy-three he'd a belly stronger than a goat's, and he'd sing his way home from King's bar every night on his old wobbly bike. And be first abroad next day. It's the way with those that are widowers young.

My mother didn't hold with Granda's easy ways. She prodded me back to work and glared at the smoking men. For all they cared. "There'll be devils enough tapping at

Val Mór's window," she snapped at them. "He'll call for his priest at the end, you'll see."

"Dolly, be easy," said my dad.

"Ah woman, that Val's no more feared of the Devil than Finn McCool was," said Granda, spitting in our clean ditch. "You womens have longer memories than Gabriel himself. And less forgiveness," he added feelingly.

My mother sniffed and told me not to stand gawping.

"We'll go up so to his house after milking," my dad declared, and when Mother said, "You will not take Stephen," he told her it would do me no harm in the world. "And you women will wait your turn till he's safe out of the world."

My granda cackled like an old gander and put his pipe away.

"As for long memories," said my dad, carefully shaving a walnut baccy plug with his old pocket-knife, "Tresa Reilly has lived to close his eyes after all."

My mother glared at all of us.

Tresa Reilly lived with her brother over in Knock town-land. Rightfully her name was Goram, Val Mór's wife, but she dropped it when he put her by.

Val Mór lived in his nephew's house, Val Beg. He was a gaunt, staring man in his eighties, very active. We children would talk at night of the old man coming after you with his long fingers, and scare ourselves under the bed-clothes. But he was friendly, though fearful sharp, and he'd be often in our kitchen, smoking and staring in the fire, for all my mother's disapproving.

The great thing with Val Mór was that he'd killed a man. Back at the beginning of the century when our lands all belonged to Major Graham, he'd staved in the head of a tinker called Rafter and had been fifteen years in Galway Gaol.

My granda remembered him coming back. Right in the middle of the troubles. "He gets down from the cart, there, at the cross, and Tresa steps out into the road with all of us watching and the troopers too. 'Forgive and Forget, Val a'sthore', she says, 'Forgive and Forget.' He lugs down his little case from the cart and 'I'll forgive you woman and forget you too, the day I see you laid on your brother's table with coins on yez eyes.' "

Big Val made good in the hard times, and he and his nephew had forty acres of the finest land when his time came.

When we got to his door that evening there was a crowd before us. You could tell by the bicycles and the dogs sniffing all round each other. Val's big collie lay by the step and none of them went near *him*.

Val Beg wasn't there but Packy Goram was and Peadar Cullin and Sean Cahill with his brothers. Our priest, Father Cosla, was sat importantly by the fire. The only other child there was my cousin Mourteen. I sat with him on the floor by the dresser, while my dad and granda found chairs for themselves.

"He'll be out soon, himself," whispered Mourteen.

"Ah no," I said. "He'll not leave his bed now."

"You'll see," said Mourteen and grabbed my kneecap tight, trying to make me laugh out loud.

My dad got two bottles of stout from the dresser. "Is it near, then, Father?" he enquired.

"He's going fast, God be praised, but he has his senses and he's for seeing you all."

There was a great fire burning there — big bricks of fine black turf, and it was close even for us two on the stone floor.

Then Val Beg comes in from the bedroom carrying his uncle and a chair all at once. It wasn't the same man at all that he'd been in the spring. He was shrunk to nothing and his cheekbones stuck out like gunwales. Still dressed in a white hospital gown under his black jacket, and his nose stretched tight as a knife on the bone. He looked like a little hawk watching, when Val Beg sat him down in the warmth.

His eyes were wickedly alive though, and his fingers were latched like ticks onto the chair arms. He was breathing heavily and sweating awful. "I see you all," he whispered, and swallowed like he had a gob stuck in his throat. "All come to see bad Val Mór go down." And he turned his head on us like an owl.

"Be easy now, Val Goram," said the priest. "We're none of us thinking any such thing. It's a better place you're heading for."

"See here Father," he snapped, and his little child's body was suddenly strong again. "I let you here because you're a man and a neighbour, d'you see, not as a priest. If you'll play the priest you can be gone." The effort weakened him considerably and he shrank back inside the chair. Nobody was for saying anything. Dying or not, he was in one of his contrary moods.

"You should be in bed, Val," said Val Beg over his shoulder. "There's no shame in a man lying down to die."

"I'll die as competent as any man here," the old fellow whispered. "When I'm ready."

"Ain't he a fright," said Mourteen in my ear. It was true. I was more comfortable looking at the holy pictures on the walls. If I caught *his* eye he might talk to me.

"Well we're glad, Val Mór," said Peader Cullin, "that you did come home to die. Your hospital is no place for it."

There was a murmur of agreement.

"Worse than the prison," hissed old Val, "and none of them fat little nuns would give you a feel even." He wasn't strong enough to laugh and he didn't try, but his hawkey eyes dared the company.

"The children, Val, the children," said Sean Cahill.

"Divil the children," he rapped, and I swear he was enjoying himself. "Is feeling a nun's tit a worse thing for them than seeing the pains of death?"

I tried to look away. We both did. "Whisht, you lads, come over now, d'you hear me."

Father Cosla protested but we dragged our feet towards the fire. "Near enough," said Val Mór, "You'd not enjoy the smell of me." Oh his eyes were deep. "Do you know, boys, I have blood running out of my back parts. I wonder now, would you . . . " I don't know what he was thinking of then but he broke into an ass's cough and I ran for my seat. When I looked up again his head was sagged over but his mouth had a thin smile at it.

My dad gave me a look. Everyone was very still, like they thought Val was about to die there in front of them. We all seemed to hold our breath and the smoke drifted up to the thatch to no sound but Val Mór's tattered breathing.

"It's me only sorra," he said suddenly, "that Tresa Reilly has come as far as this. I would have lasted her by, only for this feckin can-ser."

"We have to talk of that, so," said Father Cosla, spreading his big hands on his knees. He was a local man and a strong one and he'd the devil's own nerve, for a priest. Which was why Val Mór abided him. "It's time now you took back your bad word. Now, now, you don't have to see her, Val: I would take your message with gladness."

Val Mór narrowed his eyes and stared at him.

"Tis the only thing lying on your conscience, Val," Sean Cahill broke in, rushing his words. "Your crime is paid for in full."

The old chest heaved a dozen times as he tried to speak. But it came clearly enough when he started. "Crime, Crime?" he said. "They threw trash into the cell with me that had killed better men than Tim Rafter, and with less reason, and now they're famous patriot hayroes."

"Tis different, Val, tis different," said Cosla soothingly. "But we won't talk of it now anyways. Tis long done with."

"Tis no different and we *will* talk of it," said Val. "See you *Father* Jimmy Cosla," and the scorn was considerable, "though it cannot happen to you; and see *you* Sean Cahill, because it *may* come your way. If you come home from the bog, and take your wife to the bed, and then you find," he paused, leant forward and panting, "that you've to wash another man's scum off your purogs . . . "

My dad was on his feet, though my granda was laughing silently in pure happiness. My dad took Mourteen and myself as far as the gate only. "Straight home, now, yous," he ordered, "and not a word to your mams do you hear."

"Ain't death a grand thing," said Mourteen as we went over Saint Colman's stream.

Val Mór's coffin was very fancy lying in the chapel that Wednesday. The church was as full as Good Friday and there were flowers galore. Weren't the women bawling happily into their shawls when Tresa Reilly comes down the aisle with a bouquet fetched all the way from Galway, and lays it on the shiny box. My mother looked very satisfied and gave over tugging my Sunday collar straight. "A sad day, Mrs. Goram," she whispered piously. My granda sat in the pew behind us and hummed a waltz tune.

Father Cosla gave Val Mór a great oration. "And the happiest thing, dearly beloved, is that all bitterness went from the old man's heart before he breathed his last. He forgave his trespassers as our Lord taught us in his own favourite prayer that we should . . . "

"Oh tis a lie, a blessed lie," my granda whispered joyfully, so my mother could hear. "Not a word of forgiveness did he breathe."

"We may be sure, my dear children, that old Val Goram can see us now gathered here and interceding for him with our prayers. And that he is at peace, at one with his maker and with his mother church.

"Oh Jasus," said my granda, much too loudly, "Cosla himself couldn't get the sacrament to Val's lips till the old sinner was already dead."

ϒ ϒ ϒ

prelude

In the tiny, featureless burial ground outside Port Clements, on the Queen Charlotte Islands, there's the grave of a man who identifies himself as a US Cavalry soldier. It's a lonely thought.

He was the germ of Charley Wesley in this story. (Naming him for the author of "Hark The Herald Angels Sing" was simple mischief on my part. Perhaps.)

It fascinates me, and makes me dizzy, to imagine just how much one lifespan has been able (or unable) to comprehend in the 100 years since the world speeded up. (Ah, you must have seen some changes in your time.) I wrote one story, "Cross Fox", about a Métis teenager from Saskatchewan who is sent to the Boer War as an alternative to a prison sentence. From there he moves to England, fights in WWI, and ends up as sexton in an English country churchyard, telling his story to his WRAF great-niece as the German bombers drone overhead towards Coventry.

Charley Wesley's life has been almost as busy. But he has only his memories to define himself by, and his desperate, outrageous behaviour, his need to be a "bad boy" to the end, support the most courageous stand the old warrior has ever made.

He's blessed though, I think, in two things. Firstly, he's in a "cottage hospital", allowed to be a "character": loved, teased and acknowledged. There's no high-tech machinery here, but there is humanity and healing.

Secondly he has what he most needs in his final loneliness — a comrade, the old Haida gentleman in the next bed.

And this story is really more Joshua Young's than Charley's. The world old Josh knows is tiny in space — the islands — but infinitely rich in time: the generations, before and after him, flowing together. This is, and will be, his home. He has the weary serenity that the Bardo Thodol, the Tibetan Book of the Dead, assumes in its last injunction: Let go, let go . . .

What delays that letting go is his humanity. He worries, as all good old people must, about the changing world and his family's ability to weather it. And he cares, and worries, about Charley. Perhaps there is something yet to be done for the old soldier's spirit . . .

There's a passage in "Deathbed" where the old men's thoughts take on a life of their own, as two flies circle above them in the silent room. Originally their voices blended into one but, despite my Dutch friend's enthusiasm, I now find that passage too hard to follow. It breaks the spell it was intended to strengthen. The new version is less "experimental" and much clearer.

The image of the killer whales entering Masset Inlet comes perilously close to what Samuel Beckett called "jewel theft" — using other peoples' secrets to add spice or pretended insight to one's work. I believe that my Haida friends will feel my real love for old Josh and his family, and accept that the whales should be there.

DEATHBED

With the whispering rattle of seeds on a drum they were taking the old man home. A soft background, like rain upon a tent, and behind that again the tapping of a bone stick on another drum beyond the circle's edge. It went to his heartbeat, insistent but sometimes faltering: *dum, dum, dum-check, didum. Dum, dum* . . . But somehow between him and that beat, the slithering, whispering hiss of the little red seeds upon the stretched skin. As they swayed in their squatting circle, out in the shadows, to take him home.

You could not hear this in the room. The sound of the fan, the distraction of footsteps in the corridor, a truck backing up in the parking bay — everyone else heard those things. Just as the room was washed out, shadowless, by the strip lights and withheld the sun as it melted the last snowbanks out on the wooded islands of the inlet.

He had not spoken for two days. His patient, embarrassed relatives could not see in the open mouth the soul fighting its way out at last. He had lived in the worst age, through three generations, using up his energy to live.

When you had passed the point of simply living, it was time to die. Why should there be a waiting period; why did people pray for time to consider?

Unlike the other patient in the room he lay impassive, his eyes scarcely moving through the blank moments. The pale, peaked features sat strangely on the full Indian face . . .

"Goddamned Paiutes whaddya expect!" Bolt upright in bed, Charles Wesley raved at the empty room.

"Let you down every time," his voice fell into a mutter. "Son of a gun, son of a gun," he mumbled. His arms jerked up and flapped before his face. "Friggin eejits," he crowed. In the other bed his companion lay motionless, breathing softly through his open mouth, his eyes fixed on the windows, ignoring.

Charley, a gaunt old vulture at death's door, fierce and foolish. His head jerked round, the strung tendons of his neck quivered beneath the stubbled, jutting old jaw. "Hey, Josh, goddammit, snap out of it. Show a leg for Christ's sake. They're all gone y'know."

The other did not move.

"Friggin Paiutes anyway." Charley was ex-US Cavalry. He'd seen things done to native women in the nineties you wouldn't believe. Charley didn't take it personally. They were all Paiutes to him. "Paiutes!"

He saw the dark Indian eyes slide round towards him, out of their trance, glinting with humour. Charley was a fingerhold on life and he knew it.

"There you go, chief," he roared, the thin old voice breaking into a triumphant treble. "We'll give 'em hell!"

He turned back towards the door, old fingers jerking at the hem of his sheet. "Nurse," he yelled, "Nurse, goddammit, I need the bed pan." He chuckled, his head swinging like a pigeon's. "She'll take her time, Josh, she won't hurry."

A quiver of rage ran through his laughter. "Nurse," his voice failed him, "NURSE!" No sound from the corridor. "All right," he announced, "if that's the way you want it." He tugged at the blankets, twitching them by degrees clear of his body. "I can't wait, Nurse, I gotta piss." He fumbled at the cord of his hospital pyjamas and lay back.

"One, two, three and *there* she blows!"

Just below the strip lights two flies circled steadily. They held to the very centre of the room, almost as though they were lured by the ghost of a vanished, old-fashioned light-bulb.

One fly moved with the clock; the other against it. Their orbits were almost identical. In the doorway crouched the nurses' grey cat, its yellow eyes following the flies insistently and with infinite patience.

Sometimes, as their paths crossed, it looked as though they had collided and bounced away in opposite directions; and if you watched them for long enough you could not tell one direction from the other, you could not tell which fly was which. They never faltered, circling on through the evening above the two silent beds, their paths distinct and mingling.

And all who died of cancer — Minnie and Archie's Jenny with the baby just born — it seems to be taking everyone just now, like the smallpox. Scarlet fever. Joe Ball too down at the wharf. White men too . . .

Dammit children too, now that wasn't right. No, the old body just wearing down like this — you watch yourself, you're lucky. Pain was the thing. You couldn't think, not with pain.

There's been pain . . .

Those two days with my hand trapped when the log slipped down in the cabin wall. God yes, remember the ravens yelling the first morning, buggers didn't care. Me praying for anything to get free, would have cut my fingers off if the axe hadn't been lying out of reach. Turns to pride though, pain don't remember, same as the women labouring . . .

say you remember childhood things —
fish camp on the Yakoun . . .canal-side walls in Manchester . . .
they got it wrong . . . why worry . . .

Soldiering, no, didn't fit in, won't remember that, came north, no such damn thing as borders then . . .

Young Chuck, living in Alaska, call him American, fighting for them in Japan. Marine uniform, teaching his kid the old language. No sense. Too late . . .

Well, I fitted here, made my cabin didn't I, the best, made the road alone with the wheelbarrow. Great machines now. Diggers. Youngsters all gadgets. Couldn't do what I did, think I'm an old fart. Better man . . .

Young Jimmy's a good boy — cares — last summer was it taking me in his little boat to Kiusta. Asking questions all the time, old questions. Better forgotten. Good boy, though — Marv said he was Dingaan come back. Yes, swamped in the squall off Naikoon trapped in the kelp, sank. Yes, Jimmy's a good boy. Carry my coffin please . . .

Paiute cut his throat, what the hell's his name — Pinkey was it, Pinson, come back if I don't think about it. Scotchman. Got his watch. Damn, could have been me. It's all luck . . .

White girls after him all the time. All turned around. Brought that one down to the village the night we got back from our trip. Pretty little thing, what's she doing. Didn't do nothing in that room, we knew, just laid there. All turned around. One of them'll get him though, he doesn't want no native girl. Can't fathom it . . .

You work so damn hard, got no time for the women — just after a battle. Different. And the one on the train in Vancouver, should have brought her up. No, got in the way. Time you got time for it you can only think. Pisspot. Nurse . . .

No, I'm tired of thinking, it's been done, just take me home. Thinking's all hard lines. Believe anything. All good people. Just the times. Will I come back?. Uncle knows. Don't want to. Enough . . .

Thinking thoughts. Scary goddammit. Tears. Friggin' pisspot. Nurse . . .

The other doctors were assigned to the islands by the church authorities. They came for one year practicums and left. Rachel Bennet was here of her own choice. She had her own practice and an office in the old customs shed, and she had bought a house. She was small, determined, brusquely efficient, but her world was not bounded by medical science. She was trusted, quickly adopted by the people, ringing true to the sixth sense that all islanders have, and to the seventh sense of the natives.

She chatted leisuredly to the old man, as though she had no schedule beyond this room, looking always at his eyes where the life was and taking for granted, though he lay immobile, that there was something between them. Mary, his niece, stood beside her, large and imperturbable. The doctor talked to her through Josh instead of the other way around. That counted among them.

"Your family want you home, Mr. Young." He would have nodded if he could. "I don't know if we're doing you very much good here . . . I know Mary would do as well by you as our nurses." His eyes shifted fractionally to his niece. Mary had been such a nervous, sickly little girl — now she was strong, accomplished, mother to five. "Now you have to tell her, Mr. Young, that she's needed at home."

Because that no good Cyril was drinking again, he'd lose his boat again, he didn't deserve her. "She won't leave here till you do, you know that . . . I'm going to talk to Dr. Kyle about it tonight." It didn't matter to him like it should, but he knew it was right. "All right?" His eyes were eloquent, but tired.

"Nice pair of tits that girl," Charley announced smugly to the world at large. "Never seen a sawbones like that before."

Mary snorted with laughter — "He is a case."

Dr. Bennet was not perturbed: "He just wants his share of attention, that's all."

Charley sprawled owlishly on his pillow. "Whassamatter? You *have* got a nice pair of tits. For a doctor." He wheezed after his next words: "Man can't help his eyes can he?"

The young doctor crossed to his bed. "He could help his tongue perhaps, Mr. Wesley."

"Yes, you tell him," said Mary stormily.

"Eh?" he quavered. "Dammit, I'm too old for pernickity finnickies. Your fault for surrounding us with dames. Man's world," he growled. "Why've I got to lie here and have you all waving your tits around? Not my fault."

"Well, how have you been, Mr. Wesley?"

"You know as well as me. Take my pulse, do something useful godammit. Bunch of females." Charley was off on one of his rants.

"It won't be age or sickness that carries *you* off, Charley," said the doctor firmly. "One of these days that temper of yours is just going to be too much for you."

She called to the little Filipino nurse from the doorway. "Sally, can you tidy Mr. Wesley's bed up a little — he's wrecked it again."

"Don't worry about me, girl," Charley raved. "I'll outlast old Josh there — man's got no spirit, gives up. Same with all Paiutes, y'know." He squinted at the nurse: "Little squaw like you, now — no damn spirit — all *yes doctor, no doctor,* eh? Paiutes!"

Mary loomed at him in outrage. "You Charley Wesley, you old goat, you couldn't tell a Hottentot from an Eskimo."

"All Paiutes," said Charley happily

He watched the nurse covertly for a few moments, still as a chastened child, while she tucked in the sheets. His watery blue eyes gloated down the neck of her white dress. There the dark little breasts perched upon the firm cotton hammocks of her brassiere. He knew that she knew, and the doctor too. That was his privilege.

"Goddammit," he exploded as she stood up and turned to Joshua's bed. "You just want to cut my balls off, same as the rest of them." He humped over sulkily, turning his scrawny back on them.

"Come off it, Charley," the doctor said, "I'm a doctor, not a vet." They were both laughing as she left the room; the ghost of a cackle rose from his pillow. "Goodnight, Mr. Young," she said quietly from the door.

The habit of speech had left him. He appreciated his niece and the doctor, and Charley's defiant ribaldry, but as if from a great distance. Whenever there was silence he could hear the breathing of the drummers out in the darkness; but when people were coming and going and getting exercised, he just watched them with a calm affection. The streams came down to the pool from too many sources — he could not concentrate on them. He was not engaged.

Charley would pester him at night, breaking through the entrancing shadows with no concern for the clock. Tonight the beams from Sandspit lighthouse were flicking and darting up the inlet at long intervals.

"You people believe in it, don't you, Josh? This *incarnation*." In the dark room Charley's throaty words were spooky, they hinted at a death rattle. "That's why the people don't care so much — your Mary don't care like she should, Josh. Is that why, HEY?"

Charley clamoured. The night nurse spoke irritably from the door: "Settle down, Charley, people have to rest."

"Gimme a light, nurse — black as a squaw's armpit in here."

The woman came in briskly, unfussed. "If you promise to be quiet." She switched on his bedlamp, tilting the shade so that the other bed was not exposed. "And if there's any more noise from you, I'll have your bed moved into the corridor. Mr. Young's very weak, you know."

As the rustle of her dress receded down the still corridor, Charley's sheets churned furiously. "Liar," he yelled. "Liar, liar, pants on fire," and then gave a strange little laughing cough. A few minutes later Joshua's eyes passed from the mirror window to the neighbouring bed. Charley's face was immobile, nailed to the pillow, the scared old eyes protesting the blow that had frozen him there.

Deft and unthinking as a young man's, Joshua's arm reached up behind him for the bell.

"A stroke," said the night nurse at once, "and I'm not surprised."

The old man's mouth was dry with disuse: "Will he die?" he whispered.

The nurse looked over. She showed no sign that she registered the change in him. "Oh he's a tough old bird, aren't you, Charley? Don't worry, old timer," she said gently, 'You'll be plaguing us for a good while yet.' But her eyes told Joshua differently.

Dr. Bennet was down from her house in ten minutes and worked furiously with Charley till the dawn light showed grey under the misted windows. She paused for a rest and a cup of coffee. "Oh for gosh sakes," she said incredulously. Charley's eyes were intently devouring her cleavage.

The excitement had not done him any good. He felt his strength leaving him, his blood running cold like hill water out through his feet. His legs were a ridge of slate, open to the weather. A little tremor of panic eddied in his gums with a taste of iron — soon the circle of concentration around his head, his mind, would break down and he would lose himself. The drum taps surged back at him, raggedly now, at the circle's edge. They would let him pass through them, flowing out along his legs with the last strength of his heart. He felt tears welling below his eyes at the loneliness, the great cold openness of the sky. He would be on the hillside soon. And then, as the melting snows of his body flowed around his groin, he began to enjoy it. The bliss that his great uncle, Sclikwa, had suffered for him, drowning like Dingaan off Naikoon Point.

In the evening they hooked him up again to the bottle and the tube. For blood this time, dark quarts of captive blood. His words were unlocked now, there was no use in hoarding them. His face gestured to the doctor to come close. From the pillow he whispered, "Is that white man's blood?" Rachel Bennet was caught off guard: "I imagine so, why?" He smiled shyly, "They'll never let me back to the village now," he breathed, "Can't have no half-breeds, eh?"

Out of all proportion she laughed then, and the joke went to Mary and the girls outside the door, and down the corridors to the staff room and the other wards. He had left them something — now, he knew, it was almost time to go.

Mary was called to the phone down the corridor and then they could hear her crying. A small knot of native people, related or not, drifted in from the waiting rooms to comfort her. The hospital staff kept respectfully clear.

Charley's eyes glared curiously at the door, thirsting for action. The little Filipino nurse came in and sat gently beside Joshua, touching his shoulder. "Your niece is very upset, Mr. Young," she said, her own eyes a shade wider from the mood of the corridor. She did not understand. "She wants to talk to you." Joshua nodded gravely, imperceptibly, "All right, sure," he whispered.

Mary filled the doorway, a cluster of concerned, involved faces behind her. Her great shoulders were still shaking spasmodically, her matronly Haida face held the eyes of a young girl.

"Uncle Josh," she said and she spoke loudly, publicly — it was not any more the time for effacement and Charley and the nurses did not exist. "I hope you can hear me. Jimmy just called on the phone — he says the blackfish came up the inlet this morning, four of them. He's coming down right away to get you."

A sympathetic murmur came from the group behind her; the dark women's faces held together. Joshua's left hand struggled free of the sheets — the nurse leant over to help him. He cleared his throat almost noiselessly, and moistened his lips. Hand and head, so shrunken, beckoned to his niece. She approached heavily, eyes fixed on his, and the others came behind her, standing in a strong half-circle at the bed's end. She moved to his side. Without knowing why, the nurse slipped away, almost furtively, out of the ring.

"Mary," Josh said, "Mary." She could hear him distinctly, though the others could not catch the words. She squeezed his hand — it was cold and damp under hers. "Mary, don't fret. Hmm?" She nodded, then looked round to the supporting faces. "I'm ready, Mary, don't fret. You're a good girl, Mary."

"But geez," she said, her broad face wrinkling again, "But geez, Uncle Josh, we got to get you home."

"Ah," said her friends. But would there be time?

He was so close to the circle's edge now, in a moment he would see their faces, would be able to talk to them. The figures were distinct now, the seed drum dipping and sifting in their hands under the clusters of red seeds. Only the shadows that fell across their faces kept them back. He

48

could almost touch the man in front of him, and he prepared to seize his arm across the drumskin and bring his face close, knowing him, as soon as he had drifted just a little closer. There was a light somewhere to the West, throwing the shadow. He was moving as a tree grows, steadily, imperceptibly into the light.

He woke up. He was not expecting it. He did not want it. But, without effort, he accepted. The sky beyond the windows was almost clear and the late morning sun angled at the room, cut off partly by the drapes. He looked straight out at the sky but Charley was in clear view, too, beside him. Charley, profiled rigidly against the sky, shifting his faller's axe dubiously, eyeing the deep back-cut in the young cedar. A ridge-pole for his cabin, likely. Charley who outlived him and would be gone, then, forever into the rootless dark.

There was a small, nagging shadow between him and the sun, somewhere out over Haina ridge. It hung there steadily, like a mote in a forest light-shaft, like an insect hovering. Perhaps he closed his eyes again. The nearest drummer was breathing softly, just beside him. It was a friend, yes, an old friend, but he could not see him yet. Whether his eyes were open or not, the window was there still, and the space across the inlet where that speck was moving closer. It must be a bird, its wings fixed in a long slow glide towards his room. He knew that he must wait for it, must pass the last test of patience.

Foxed by the screen around the bed, Charley strained his ears towards the doorway.

"Mary, there's no question of it," said Dr. Kyle.

"That's for us to decide," said Jimmy. "I got a cab waiting!"

Dr. Bennet's voice broke in: "It really is impossible, Jimmy. He would die in the car — you could take the ambulance for that matter, it would be the same. He might die as you were carrying him out."

The people in the corridor shifted and muttered unhappily — they did not want this scene. Jimmy hesitated, but he had screwed himself up to this.

Dr. Bennet said quietly, before he could speak, "Mary, Jimmy, listen — you would *hurt* him."

It was the slowness across that distance that was so difficult: how to stay with that relentless, hour-hand approach.

You wanted to hurry it because you were a man; you wanted to cut out the bits that were understood and could be taken for granted; you wanted to imagine the distances crossed in a second; only the beginning and the end counted to a man.

But you were not allowed. He saw a water-drop hanging from the tap in his kitchen, but the tap was not allowed. Lingering snot from his grandmother's nose, that was all right. He saw his son, Alec, blowing and blowing, red-faced at a balloon that grew impossibly large, hiding his face, and the whole room tense for the explosion. But that was not allowed — the colours in the balloon, the screaming, vibrating yellows and blues were wicked. The garish, painted colours and rhythms of the century were smothering him, scattering across the clear skin of the drum. He threw them off with his last strength and trampled them. He understood now. He watched the tide at Blue Jackets inching upon the grey stones under the forest. That was it. He fixed his eyes upon the bird.

It was much closer now. After all, it was not gliding. Its wings were bringing it down to him fast. He realised how large it was, blotting out the hills of the inlet as it came to the window in a sudden rush.

The white owl hung there, its yellow eyes upon him, hovering at the window. At every beat of its great moth wings it drew darkness in around it. The wings beat and beat outside the glass, their soft rush whispering like the seeds upon the stretched skin. His friend was at his shoulder now and the wings brought the darkness in, in, till the yellow eyes faded and there was nothing left but the snow-flecked breast of the bird where the drum whispered and the man's heart answered at last.

prelude

There's a bird in T.S. Eliot's poem, "Burnt Norton", which calls "Go, go," to the children in the garden: "human kind can not bear very much reality."

I wonder if that thrush was somewhere at the back of my mind when I wrote this story. For the Merchant is a realist, or would consider himself one: a man of business, power, responsibility . . .

Yet with the death of his wife, what sense of reality can he fall back upon? He enters a country of signs, as we all are likely to when beset by grief, fear, illness or isolation.

In that country, the wild things seem to speak to us. Déjà vus and previsions are commonplace. Everything has the luminosity of a dream. A complete surrender to it can lead to obsessive madness (I have seen it happen), but those signs can heal, too, and remind us not only that "there are more things in heaven and earth, Horatio, than are dreamed of in your philosophy," but also that we once understood the world in ways that we have forgotten — or perhaps dismissed as childish and fanciful.

I think the Merchant recovers his childhood. That is what heals him.

He returns to his job of course; he must — it is the life he has made for himself. But is he the same man? Not really. He has understood Death's place in Life, if only for an instant. He will not be ambushed again.

You need not take literally his wife's soul entering a bird, only to die shortly afterwards in a "nature red in tooth and claw." All the same, that second death does give him the peace she would have wished for him. Those who are leaving this world feel a terrible protectiveness towards those who remain.

My childhood did not include the mythology and rituals of the summer cottage. They seemed so exotic and affluent to me when I first came to Canada. A lot of writing has come out of that annual retreat to the Canadian Shield, and some of the stories are wonderful rites of passage. (Has anyone ever compiled an anthology?)

In the mid 1980s I was loaned such a place — Blewitt's Island on Lac La Ronge in northern Saskatchewan, where I didn't see a human being for two months. I was not dealing with death, but the end of a relationship can be a death of the spirit. I spent two weeks exorcising my personal desperations (and there were signs galore), and the rest of the time being a child, in the state of constant and attentive wonder that all writers, surely, crave. I will never forget the slightest detail of that place.

I know that a part of me will linger there forever.

THE MERCHANT

The merchant sat late in his office, staring through his own reflection at the bank highrise opposite, where Filipino and Chilean women went, floor by floor, cleaning the offices.

He walked from the business district and stopped at two bars where the waiters' familiar deference soured on him, and then he stood in a tile-floored tavern, politely deflecting the bartender's overtures and staring into the mirror behind the bar at the young people drinking and talking; bemused by their clothes, the tribal music, their irrelevance to his world.

He did not go back for his car but walked home. Through districts rising and falling in tone, past renovations, demolitions, re-zonings, between old money, new money, no money.

A two hour walk. For the last half hour, he saw not a living soul.

The only light on his street, bar the illuminated doorbells, was his own porchlight.

A decanter and glass waited on a rosewood tray in his study. He poured a drink and sat in his usual chair. The walk, instead of lifting his spirits and clearing his mind, had left him restless, uneasy.

He flicked through the TV channels with the switch on his chair arm. The talk shows and reruns from other time zones would not come into focus. He left his drink unfinished, went upstairs and changed in the bathroom, and went to bed.

His wife stirred and murmured a question in her sleep. He squeezed her hand, then turned on his side, staring through the gap in the drapes.

He had not been sleeping well. The business he had built up by skilful delegations of power was stagnant, and seemed out of his reach. With no belief in a god or an afterlife, he had taken to whispering the child's bedtime prayer: *And if I die before I wake . . .*

Other men at his age were losing their heads over younger women. He knew two or three who had done that. Ashes in their mouths after two years. The sad revenges of their wives.

Some thwarted part of him was robbing his sleep, but he did not know what it was.

He lay, sweating slightly, till birdsong and light came together at the window, and then he slept.

When he woke he could hear the hum of the city, and the sun was high outside. His wife had neglected to wake him. When he sat up she was still in bed beside him.

She was dead, and already cold.

After the funeral his older son said, "Dad, remember that loss takes time to absorb. The grieving process is a slow one." His children used language like that, but did it help *their* lives? "Be easy on yourself, Daddy," his daughter told him.

He walked in the back garden, between the rosebeds and the rockery his wife had created. He seemed not to have been there for years — the weeping mulberry tree and the flowering cherry had grown taller than him. Her flowerbeds were never geometrical; there were no ranks of colour. And the rockery was home to wildflowers and stones she'd brought down from the cottage.

He wandered in the garden like a stranger. A hermit thrush sang at intervals through the afternoon, from the bamboos behind the pond. His wife's spirit was in the bird, and she loved him more than she ever had in their time together.

He felt guilt, as his children had told him he would. Inside the house he was stricken by the vividness of his wife's disappointments and her endless, he'd thought naive, cheerfulness. A kind of faith.

He slept in the room that had been their younger son's. Where three or four times in their marriage he had withdrawn, cold and unwilling to bend, and slept alone. The memory was unbearable.

Yet he slept well, with no night-terrors or sweating, without the childhood prayer, and woke very early to the smell of rain drying, and the thrush's sweet, repetitive call,

He called his daughter and asked her to keep an eye on the house; he was going up to the cottage for a few days. She approved, relieved perhaps that he did not ask her to come. He did not call the office. The business would run by itself, and the directors had asked at the funeral that he take some time off.

He drove his wife's car north. Listened to the classical music station her radio was tuned to, till the signal grew faint, and then drove in silence.

He was conscious that he was not thinking about work, not in any detail. As his business had diversified, the commodities had become increasingly abstract. One girl he had hired twelve years ago on a hunch, ran a branch now which dealt exclusively with "futures". Sugar or palm oil, coffee, pulp, nickel — none of it actually passed through their hands. That branch had no warehouses, and it made the most profit.

As he turned from the gravel road down towards their lake, he suddenly yearned for old age.

The shutters were off the cottage, for his wife had been up twice already this year. He was aware again, poignantly, of his strangerhood. After the first few years he had come only infrequently, though each summer he promised himself, and them, that he'd come for a month. Perhaps two weekends in the year he'd drive up, and then he would bring work with him, and fret for the phone and the papers.

Everything here was his wife's making. She and the children had explored and named the different parts of the lake, and had blazed the trails, drawn the big map on the kitchen wall, stocked the small library. And for seven or eight years now she had come up alone, or had a woman friend visit at weekends. Last year she had hosted a women's retreat.

He had not been here for three years.

He slept in the big Danish bed, or on the chaise in the screen porch. The country air was soporific and the northern lights, flaring each night across the lake, tugged at some part of him like a call to hibernation. He played records from his wife's collection, till the batteries ran low. This was the kind of music, he thought, he should have piped through his offices; but then, as he listened to the water on the rocks, he began to wonder if he'd see those offices again.

His larger travel-case stayed in his wife's car, back at the head of the trail. His fishing rod lay in the back seat. When he walked round the lake on his third day, he was conscious he followed paths that she must have made, and as he rested upon a granite outcrop, polished by glacial action and warm from the days sun, he looked back at the cottage and knew this must be a favourite seat of hers. He heard the hermit thrush call again, from the osiers by the swimming cove. The spirit of his wife had followed him, and sang out of love and consolation.

He dragged the canoe down to the jetty below the cottage, and sat for an hour staring into the water. The flash of a minnow's belly drew his eyes down through the weeds. Slowly he learned to make out the paler stones on the lake bottom, and then the whole submerged landscape. The foam-flecks on the surface, the drifting leaves and the sky's reflection, all became blurred, irrelevant, at last invisible.

He began to learn every part of the property. He ate sparingly from his wife's stockpile of food in the cupboards, and used books from the library and the binoculars he had bought for her years back and which hung by the door where their children's heights and ages were marked off on the jamb, to identify birds and stars he had never noticed before, and to give them names.

After a while his daughter came up to see him. They spent an awkward evening together and he sent her away, assuring her he was all right. When she'd left he swept out the cottage and cleaned the windows, and walked all round the lake, counterclockwise.

Where the larger stream flowed from the woods he found a poplar tree felled by beavers. He picked up one of the woodchips from the grass and chewed it as he watched the unafraid creatures come back and drag segments of branches up to their conical lodge. He remembered the woodcarving set that his wife had bought him, the Christmas they had all spent up here. It was still in a drawer, in the bookcase.

That night he took out the tools and sharpened them on the stone provided, though only one chisel had ever been used, for an hour at most. And he remembered the blocks of hardwood she had bought for him too, as gifts from the children, and he retrieved one, a fine-grained maple, his younger son's gift, from the loft of the woodshed.

Wood, of one sort or another, took over his time. He felled dead trees with an axe and swede saw, working at leisure, more than once towing a trunk back behind the canoe, to be cut into stovelengths on the tressels beside the woodshed. He took a boy's delight in the work, and in the prospect of work each morning; he scouted the woods for suitable timber and planned the route home with it. He fostered a miniature empire — logging off hills and valleys, his mind emptied out of everything else. His palms became blond with calluses, his stomach fell away so much that he tied in the waist of his ragged trousers with a length of string. The woodshed began to fill, he had not heard an engine of any sort for three weeks — only, when the wind came from the south, the lagging thunder of jets high above, going down towards Toronto.

For an hour or so every evening, after bathing and shaving by the dock, he worked on the maple block, shearing and gouging patiently at the hard wood, breathing in time to his work. He left his own litter of wood chips around the granite seat, cutting a sort of waist into the block, an hourglass shape, thinking of nothing, as the hermit thrush sang from the osier beds, but the strokes into the heartwood, with no end-shape in mind.

His daughter came up with his older son, anxious, saying he had stayed long enough, appalled by his thinness. He allowed her to cut his hair, and sent them away. He could not bear the thought of them staying the night. When he looked at the file of things his son had brought up from his office, he felt dizzy. He put it, unopened, away in a closet.

The maple block became two separate cones of wood. He worked on them one at a time, every evening at the rock until there was nothing left of them but the chips on the ground, sleek and uniform.

He sang songs from the musicals they had listened to when they first married, carrying all the parts — happy and ridiculous in the sunlight, knowing that no eyes but the wild things' watched him, himself his own mocking audience.

He found a pair of jeans in the back bedroom. They belonged to his younger son and they fitted him now, once he had rolled up the legs. The same day he caught his reflection in the big window, with the lake behind him, and he took all his clothes off and stared at himself, wondering at the changed proportions of his body, at the imperceptible shelf at his navel, and the grey and black hairs below it. He walked on the stones with bare feet. He began to have thoughts about women, though he knew that the image of his wife would swim between him and any woman, that her voice would echo, even in fantasies.

He sharpened and oiled the carving tools one last time before folding them into their leather satchel. He sat on the granite seat with the axe, spitting upon its edge, matching the birdsongs with the measured rasp of his whetstone. A bird swooped over the cottage roof and close by his shoulder; he felt the breath of its wings. It plunged among the osiers and the hermit thrush ended her song. Astonished, he saw the grey hawk pressing its victim down into the dry moss, its wings and legs flex and the thrush's tail flare beneath it. He felt something tighten in his chest, as if he were there, not here. In that moment the complex scent of the lakeshore seemed to breathe into him. Death had a sudden clarity. The hawk glared over its shoulder at him and then flew off across the water, the little thrush clutched in one fist. It settled upon a half-dead pine he'd marked out for his woodshed, above the beaver dam.

The merchant put down his axe and walked to the spot where the hawk had dived. He picked a brown, mottled feather from the moss and twirled it slowly between thumb and finger. It was warm — from the sun or from the bird's life? The mystery and the simplicity overwhelmed him. He went into the cottage and got his wife's field glasses. The hawk ate slowly, its neck graceful as a snake, plucking the down from its victim's breast, drawing out meat at leisure. The merchant watched until it was done, the glasses twitching from the pulse in his wrists. Curled feathers drifted upon the stream, out to the lake. The hawk flew off to another tree, preened itself and settled to sleep. He stood there for more than an hour, and it did not stir. He went back to the cottage exhilarated.

That evening a storm came down on the lake, knocking two trees down, close to the cottage. He lay in the screen porch, a child's delicious dream of danger, as though he were out at sea, and when it was done he lay watching and listening to the calm recover his lake, the half moon on the settling water, the little waves muttering at the rocks, pale strands of light whipping the horizon as the clouds broke away.

All around him the woods dripped loudly into the underbrush. His blanket was damp from the rain that had blown into the porch. He leaned up on the chaise and stared until his eyes made an abstraction of the night, and the screen's mesh came into focus. He was mesmerised by the tight grid of the wires, lit vaguely from behind by the moon's diffused light off the water. Their geometry became a maze through which small atomic ciphers zigzagged. Before he had married he had been in the habit of making lists at his night table, of setting things in order for the next day before he would let himself sleep. The simmering fabric behind his eyelids had danced as the screen did now, towards some order, and he would turn on his lamp again, or write in the darkness — reminders, resolves, inspirations.

The nagging question of the grain futures surfaced from an age ago. It was not really his concern, but he'd been uneasy. They had taken them up only because the price was absurdly low. The old motto came back from his college days — *stumbling blocks* and *stepping stones*, yes. And with things turning out as they were in Europe, he could see it suddenly — a whole new enterprise, action, and his younger son, the boy whose jeans he was wearing now, whose mother had indulged him and packed him off to Korea to study pottery, the boy would come back some day, with his flair for languages, yes, and he'd take it over. The merchant could hardly wait for the night to end.

In the morning he dragged the canoe up and hoisted it into the woodshed roof. He scrubbed his hands, locked up the cottage, and drove his wife's car out from the fireweed and brambles that had grown up past its fenders. He stopped for lunch at the hotel in Huntsville, his first glass of wine in a month. The writing in his appointment book was that of a tired old man; the meetings he had missed, the convention, the trade show seemed now the lazy gestures of someone on the verge of replacement. Before driving on he bought a suit, off the rack, from the menswear store; was amused to realise that he filled the cubicle with the odour of woodsmoke and wet wool.

He tuned the radio to a Detroit news station. Every report had a different slant on the future, and few made sense. He could have been Rip Van Winkle.

Twenty miles down the two-lane highway, a Mennonite buggy pulled out from a sideroad. The merchant's view was blocked by the tractor-trailer ahead, and when it swerved wildly he found himself bearing down on the carriage at 70 miles an hour, the driver's face, under her ribboned black bonnet, a mask of stolid alarm, the horse plunging.

He swung his wheel as he braked, and the car turned around on the gravel verge, slid backwards into the ditch and onto its side, and crushed its rear end against a telephone pole.

He climbed out and stood in the sunshine, talking to the woman, patting the trembling horse, while the truck driver pulled out his bags and papers from the car.

The police cruiser drove him on south. "I feel as though it was my fault," he told the driver. "Be easy on yourself," the policeman said. "It takes time for the shock to wear off." He radioed ahead for a rental car, and by dusk the merchant was back in the city.

He checked in at the Four Seasons, ate a leisurely supper over the *Globe & Mail,* and walked the three blocks to his office building. The cleaners were finishing his floor as he left the elevator.

He sat at his desk, writing memos to all his executives, planning the day ahead.

prelude

I heard a child crying in a dream, and this story formed itself in the course of the next few days.

The crying became a voice, of sorts. I see most of my stories in an interior cinema, but this wanted to be a real film and I think the way it is written (the jump-cuts, the close-ups, above all the present tense) preserves that cinematic style. It was going to start with a hospital window, seen from inside, to the sound of a woman's last breaths which change, first to the "newborn" crying and then to the voice — in the Cree language with English subtitles — as the camera goes out through the city, in the half-light of dawn, and towards Terry's home.

But I'd seen too vividly what can happen to writers and their work when they engage with the film world. After one such debacle, Aldous Huxley advised writers to preserve "not the courage of your convictions so much as the obstinacy of your intuitions." So I did work it out as a story.

I realise now that Terry is embarked on a vision quest, and would be even if she had not just discovered her native origins. Visions are not found only on clifftops, in hermitages or by waterfalls, nor are they reserved for ascetics and mortifiers of the flesh; and sometimes, unsought, they seek us out instead.

In any case, the mischievous angels (or tricksters, if you prefer) who stage-manage such events are adepts of irony and ambush.

Terry's vision of herself as her mother, Maria, is completely nasty. Yet it illuminates.

"Those who have no knowledge of what has gone before them," Cicero wrote, "must forever remain children." Terry will grow up. So will her daughter.

Give the dead half a chance and they'll redefine your life!

MARIA

She knows me. She has heard me before. She must have deamed of this before I came to her. But I have never been so close. Now she contains the crying that overwhelms her. I'll be with her still, when she wakes.

I am only a cry, a child's cry of fear and foreboding inside her. I came as a cry, stretched and fearful across the grey city. I cried myself into her dream, she accommodates me.

I am greedy and I suffer inside her suffering, sucking upon her blood and her memory. I will survive.

She gasps as if there were not enough air for both us. I am at home in her. We must learn each other's names before we can become strangers.
I am crying. Her fear overwhelms me.

René's eyes open as Terry struggles beside him. She has dragged the top sheet into a rope away from him. There's just enough light from the window for him to see her, thrashing upon the pillow as though she were drowning. The fingers of one hand scrabble before her mouth like someone dying, and terrible sounds are coming out of her.

As he reaches over, the turmoil crescendoes, her moans are threaded by a thin whimpering, her hand clutches the sheet and she sits up: she is rigid and staring, it ends with a convulsive gasp.

"What is it?" he says. "What were you dreaming?"

Her head snaps round, she stares at his face, like a child in fever. Her mouth is open, her green eyes blank in their white surrounds. He strokes her shoulder; the skin is clammy.

And she flinches from his touch, pulling the sheet against her and backing away across the bed. "Easy," he says. "Easy. *Soi tranquille, hein?* It was just one of your dreams." Her eyes are in focus now, but he could still be a stranger. Her head drops sullenly, she mutters to her knees: "I always have bad dreams when you stay over." He shrugs and lies back. A blackbird starts in, outside the window. His eyes move from her face to the draped sheet — her skin there, flowing from her ribs, to her hip, to her thigh. He reaches across again.

She swings her legs off the bed: "I'll go sleep on the couch."

"It's your bed," he says, "that's crazy. I'll go."

But she's moving already, past the end of the bed towards the door. He watches the set of her shoulders, the line of her calves. He pulls the quilt over him and turns back, sighing, on his pillow. Birds are singing everywhere down the street.

At 9:30 he calls from the doorway: "You better get up. I made coffee."

She turns onto her back and smiles, sleepily. Her hand reaches out from the sheet: "Come here. Lie with me a minute."

"There's not much time," he says, but he goes over. He sits on the couch and holds her hand, but his mind's already at the office.

Her eyes seek his, her smile ingratiates: "I hate those shitty dreams. I'm sorry." She pulls the back of his hand up to her cheek. "I'm sorry. There's this one I keep having — I just can't get out of it."

Talking about it has brought tears up in her eyes. "Okay," he says, "but now you have to get up."

"Can I see you tonight?"

He laughs, short but pleased: "I imagine so, *poupée*. Why not?" She lets him kiss her at the crown of her head.

He stands up. She takes a breath and lifts her chin as though to speak, but thinks better of it. Rises instead with her usual abruptness and heads for the bathroom. She brushes past him — his hands reach for her instinctively. "I know," she says from across the hall. "I'm so young and beautiful, and I'm a pain in the ass too. You needn't say it!" He shrugs.

The hot water hisses between her shoulder blades and around her ears. She exales loudly — *Aaagh* and again, *Aaagh*, a delighted shudder passing through her legs, body, arms. She is warm all through — she turns her face into the shower's jet. The night's uneasy echoes recede, she blows into the waterfall, *Wubblebubble*, like a child, and breathes in deeply before she snaps the lever down. The water tumbles round her ankles now. She swills a wash-cloth around the bath with her foot and lets the tap run on, for it is when she bends down that the nausea comes — uncoiling from the pit of her stomach up through her throat to her face — and she delays as long as she can.

But there's nothing; she is almost reluctant to believe it. She steps from the bath and moves with a kind of elation to the washbasin, and the mirror.

There is the face that will be mine while I'm with her. It is almost familiar. The eyes and the nostrils that will let the world into me. She leans towards her reflection. What is new in her eyes? I stare back through her.

Her flesh is sweet and strong about me. I reach out for the limits of her skin. She is brave and beautiful. We will survive.

Her fingers press softly upon the mouths of her breasts.

She is singing for me.

She hears the doorbell through the water's chute in the toilet. She goes to the window, stands on tiptoe and wipes her palm through the steam on the upper pane.

Her father's car is down by the curb. Someone's looking out at the rear window. A boy? Dark face. There are voices in the kitchen.

"Shit!" She has nothing to cover herself.

She wraps the wet towel around her and goes out.

In the moment before they see her, they are two middle-aged men framed by a doorway. A snapshot of awkwardness. René has less hair than her father.

Daddy's eyes bolt from her semi-nudity. His meek hand gestures to René. Daddy's clothes and hands conspire against himself — his weakness and humility enrage her.

René starts to speak for him: "Your father says — "

"What do you want? Why did you come here?"

Her father ducks his head, his eyes come up beseechingly, wavering at her bare thighs. "I'm sorry, Terry."

"Well?" She hears, and hates, her mother in herself.

"Your mother's in the hospital, Terry," and his eyes fall away again. "I believe she is dying . . . She asked to see you."

She moves towards him: "Oh Daddy, I'm sorry. You could have phoned — you should be there . . . "

His cringing is dreadful. His eyes yearn to accept her pity, but:

"Your real mother, Terry."

Her snake eyes remind him just how much she is not his.

"René — find me a cigarette. I'm getting dressed."

She's still tugging her jeans closed when she returns: "How did she know where to find you?"

"She's always known. What could I do, Terry? — her husband sent their son round to the house. I had to come for you . . . "

"She's always known?"

"We agreed she shouldn't interfere with your life."

"You never told me you knew her."

"We agreed. She understood. Mummy and I thought it was best for you."

Terry dunks her cigarette in the cold coffee. Maybe she is going to be sick today after all.

It passes. "I'm ready."

He gets up the courage to say, "Do you think you should dress like that for the hospital?"

"Yes," she says. And sees from the door that her father is taking in the kitchen he's never seen: the ketchup spill down the stove front, the dishes by the sink, the Pizza Hut box on the floor up against the Safeway bag, angular with garbage.

Not his own cozy little hell.

René takes her arm. She kisses him brusquely. He'd like to have played it domestic. "Don't come to work, Terry," he says, "but call me if you want. I'll come around about seven. Don't get upset, *hein?*" They are public utterances. "*Au revoir*, Mr. Dawson — good to 'ave met you at last," as he closes the door. René's face can be tough, and ugly.

The car smells exactly as it did when they bought it. Clean, factory vinyl. Blister-pack seat covers. The boy huddles against the back door. "Hi," she says and reaches to pull the ashtray out. It's never been used. Her father adjusts his seatbelt, the Rotarian badge on his key ring trembles as the engine starts up. He depresses the handbrake: "This is Tony," he says.

"Hi," she says again.

Her husband sent their son round to the house — jesus: "You're my brother."

He stares back. The car moves out from the curb. Her chin is on the seat-back, she searches for herself in him: what does *he* see?

There are openings in her skin. He is almost familiar.
A dream inside a dream. He is searching too. Come in, Come in.
He is brave.

"Are there any others?" she asks. "You got any brothers, sisters?"

He mumbles something. He looks down.

"What?"

"Gracey and Alice." It's like a whisper, his lips scarcely move. He makes her feel strident.

"How old are they?"

He squints at his hands: "Seven, I guess. Alice was just five last week."

She smiles. His lips mirror politely. "I always wanted a sister," she says. "I never thought of a brother." He shrugs

— she lunges down and catches his wrist: "So, do I look like Her? How sick is She?"

He doesn't understand why he trusts her.

"She went asleep last evening." His bottom lip leads, accenting his murmuring voice: "She ain't going to wake up. Never."

He would like to tug his hand free, but he daren't. His eyes check her father. "You must be sad," she says. "I'm sorry."

They pass the plastic buffalo by the exhibition grounds. Then the brown spike of the bible college. He stares out at them.

She releases his wrist, turns to her father: "Tell me about her."

Daddy's rimless glasses, his pale hands at ten-to-two on the wheel, the sparse hairs on his knuckles, riddle her with irritation. He looks sideways for a moment, clears his throat, lifts his head to concentrate on the traffic. The message is *The boy's listening, Mummy could be listening, don't make things difficult . . .*

She whirls back again to her brother. He's backed up against the upholstery, his dirty fingernails press into the denim on his knees, the Indian face avoids hers. "I didn't know," she says. "That she was a native, I mean. That I am. I used to wonder . . . "

"My dad's Métis," he says.

He's a nice looking kid. "How old are you?"

"Eleven years."

"I'm nineteen."

"I know." There's the ghost of a real smile, but not for her.

The car pulls over. "I won't go into the parking lot, Terry." Her father rolls down his window. "I'll wait for you here."

The boy watches for her lead. "Okay," she says, and yanks at the door handle. "C'mon, Tony — you better show me the way."

Crossing the street, she almost reaches for his hand. He walks stolidly beside her. Halfway through the lot he points across her: "That's my dad's truck." A white pickup, with a fuel tank in back.

"What's his name, your Dad?"

"Jim Coulter."

"I thought Métis had French names." They start up the wide steps below the *Admissions* sign, and a dread she hasn't felt since school fumbles under her heart. Tony pulls at the big glass door: "His grandfather was Scotch. Hudson Bay Man."

She hesitates, squinting back into the sun-glare of the cars and the concrete. "Jesus, I hate hospitals," she says. "Me too" — he startles her by spitting down onto the step behind them. The spermy dreg winks from the hot cement.

It's all like TV except for the smell. Even the corridor-sounds have the tinny remoteness of TV. Hospitals, "retirement homes", prisons, schools — the quarantined communities that you never need remember. Sick flesh, old flesh, hopeless bodies with insane, important eyes. She finds that her fists are clenched, that she's walking beside her brother without drawing breath. She breathes out with a long, shuddering effort. A burst of laughter comes from a nurses' lounge to their left.

There's a man with a floor polisher, two oriental nurses carrying blankets, two sag-mouthed wheelchair-cases parked in front of a TV set, one of them sleeping. Nightmares within nightmares.

Tony moves ahead, then stops at the door of a small ward. Room for three beds. He stares at the empty one under the window. Outside, two cottonwoods and beyond them the pitch of the Roughriders' stand. A nurse steps past Terry: "She's gone, Tony I'm sorry." She's black, wavy-haired, her smile's unfeigned; she puts her arm round the boy's shoulders. He stares at the bed — it's made up, waiting. And to Terry: "You her sister? You've got the same mouth."

Terry shakes her head. Why can't she say it? "Tony's my brother."

Then: "Can I see her?"

"Surely," the nurse says. "I wouldn't suggest you take Tony, though."

"Where's my dad?" he asks, eyes still on the bed.

"He's down at the office, honey. I'll take you along for a coke just now — he has a few papers to sign."

And left, down the corridor: "You'd never think she had a girl your age."

Terry wants to hug the poor kid. She needs to. But the nurse is between them, her arm around him still; he accepts that easily. He hasn't looked at her once.

And doesn't when the nurse knocks on a green door, unlocks it herself, and holds it open. Her smile is gentle: "We'll be down at Reception. Okay?"

There's an alcove with a desk and a filing cabinet by a frosted window. A man in green fatigues, writing; there's a rubber glove on his left hand. The door closes of itself. He looks up: "Hello?"

Terry reaches for the name: "Coulter," she says. "My mother?"

He looks her over curiously. "You don't need to, you know." He strips off the glove. "Your father's signed all the papers."

"I want to."

He nods to the table beside her. She hadn't noticed. It's on castors; there's a huge double sink beyond it.

Not like TV — there doesn't seem room for a body inside the blanket's contours.

"Want me to do it?"

She shakes her head, her back's towards him already. She senses his tactful retreat to the alcove.

> I have shut myself up in her.
> There are cold winds around her.
> The grey city.
> Her skin closes against them.
> I shall sleep. I can trust her. We move closer together.

If there were a pillow under the head it would seem less unreal. There's nothing there, she's come too late, she knows this at once. The top lip falls strangely, pointed, upon the lower. Nostrils pinched. There's a hint of white under one of the eyelids. René says that her eyes roll up when she's coming.

Yes, it's a young face, young shoulders. But it's empty, casual as a cat's carcass by a ditch. The hair could be living — black like her own, but thicker, it shines a little under the strip lights. It must have been long — it disappears under the shoulders. Terry touches it, hooks a finger through it. The cheekbone is cold, unexpected; but then the room, she realises, is cold.

"What did she die of?" She turns and leans her bum on the table. The man looks over, file in hand. His eyes move from her thighs to the dead face beside her. "You don't know?"

"It's the first time I've seen her." Something about that makes sense to him.

"Pneumonia," he says. He puts the file down and comes over. How could he look at his wife's body, at his kids, after a day's work here? But his eyes aren't cold, not even indifferent. He reaches for the blanket — she gestures to stop him. "She only had one lung, you see — TB: they're pretty susceptible to it."

His pale eyes ask permission. He covers the face. Just a strand of hair lies exposed.

"I guess she wasn't too strong. And farming's a hard life. Young kids, too — shouldn't have had them really. The last one was a Caesarean."

"But she looks so young."

"Thirty-one, if you can trust the records. Yes. Guess she was just a kid when she had you?"

"I guess so."

"Adopted out, were you?"

She nods.

"Ah, well," he says. "We have to make the best of what life provides us, eh?"

Terry shakes her head, incredulous at what neither she nor the man understand. "I should go," she says. "Thanks."

"You take care now." He holds the door open for her.

She nods again. Takes a wrong turning, walks back past the green door. She could do with a beer.

She's going to tell her father to go on home; she'll walk. She stops outside the doors to light a cigarette. Finds herself looking for Tony's spittle on the step. The sun has eaten it.

I am quick. I whisper through her cells.

She is free, and breathing for me again, and I recognize what
she does not know.
I unfurl in her, we are alone and sufficient, I blossom behind her
eyes.
Ah, yes.
Life reaches towards me, I am drawn out of myself

Her eyes are drawn through the parking lot, across the
glancing light and the hot shadows. The man's face turns at
the same time. He drops his forearm from the pickup roof.
The young face at the window beside him, the white pickup.

Each takes an uncertain step but then, as she moves
cautiously down towards the ambulance bay, he heads
across. It seems to her that he controls the space between
them, so that even as his body turns and sidesteps to
thread the ranks of cars his eyes are fixed on her and his
feet never deviate. Cowboy heels, and jeans that fit snug
over his boots. He treads lightly for a big man, he com-
mands his body.

He looks up from the foot of the steps. "You're Teresa,"
he says. A tremor through her that those arms could
break her in half, but would never choose to. She goes
down till her face is level with his. The eyes look into her:
native-brown but not passive or opaque. She sees no pain.

He extends his hand. Farm hands of birth and death,
hard but not brutalised. She stands there, she senses the
hand reaching to touch her body.

You dumb bitch, she tells herself, there's just been too
much going on all at once, you're flipping out. She takes
the hand: "Terry," she says.

He nods. "Jim Coulter."

Between them the man-woman appraisal. Body and
mind in the sunlight. He nods again. She says, "I'm sorry,"

and looks down, shrugging, lets go his hand, reaches in her purse for another smoke. He watches.

"I don't know what to say." She blows smoke from the side of her mouth, away from his face, sees Tony watching from the pickup. "I mean, I want to ask you all kinds of stuff. But, like, I'm intruding right now, right?"

His eyes fix between her breasts. He folds his arms: "Ask what you want," he says. "She wanted you here."

He must have learned long ago not to be awkward with himself. He stands there, waiting, concentrated, ignoring the cars that swing close by them, the straggle of people up and down the steps.

"Christ, I don't even know her name," she says. "I meant to ask Tony."

His chin flicks up, there's a hint of defiance: "Her name was Maria. We called her Marie. Marie Metcalfe." It's final as a tombstone. He's slipping back into himself — that first spark of approval gone.

"Well, was it sudden? I mean — "

"She's been dying for two years." The words are careful, the voice curiously educated. Still no pain there. He looks at her flatly: "She was never well, since I knew her."

"How old was she then? When was that?"

"Come over to the truck," he says. "I don't wish to leave Tony alone." She follows at once. He looks ahead as he speaks: "She came to me when Tony was four."

"He's not her son, then?"

"Yes, he came with her."

"So he's not yours."

"He has my name."

He carries his hardness so easily. He robs her of her own poise. She moves quickly, to keep up with him, wishes he'd notice her. He stops as a car backs out in front of them. "Who'll look after him?" she demands. "And the girls — Gracie, isn't it, and — "

"They stay with their Auntie," he says, impatient, and steps round the fender of a panel van. She has to hurry again.

"My mother's sister?"

He turns back — it must be contempt on his face: "My sister. Marie had no family."

She's only half following the words. She wants to play this *right* in his eyes. His jaw-tilt again: "We didn't talk about her family. She saw her mother in the city sometimes; I didn't meet her. Maria didn't go to the funeral. She had no time for her father."

They're beside the pickup. Tony's eyes are fixed on his father's face.

"Where were they from, Jim?" There's a weakness in using his name. He doesn't accept it: "Hartley," he says. "He ran the store." And, as he heads round to the driver's side: "I wouldn't go up, there's nothing there for you."

"What about your place? Nothing for me there either?"

He turns and places one hand on the hood ornament, a leaping silver ram: "You should just leave things be," he says. "Get on with your life, Terry."

His eyes take in her neckline and trace the side of her face. They linger on her hair. Tony's face, just two feet away, is averted.

"Couldn't I come out sometime — see Tony and the girls? I mean, they are my sisters."

"I don't see what that would achieve." He moves again and opens the pickup door. "Look after yourself, Terry."

"Well, fuck you too," she says, quiet and venomous, and turns on her heel. Then thinks, in mid-stride, she should speak to Tony.

Coulter hasn't moved. "I apologise," he says, and loses no strength in saying it. "Her funeral is on Saturday. Two o'clock in Lebret. You will be welcome."

She does not move till they've driven off. Coulter touches his hat. She winks at Tony; his hand lifts in a tiny wave.

I have to learn what she has to learn. She has to learn what I know.

Her shadow overtakes mine in this empty place.

We cast the same shadow under the sun-wheel.

Terry lights another cigarette. The sun is merciless. She's going to stop in at the Horseshoe Tavern and look at some natives, eavesdrop. Jesus, she thinks, jesus, son of a bitch, this is unreal.

And by the time she reaches the car she has changed her mind again.

Daddy is making tidy annotations in his CAA book. She gets in beside him: "I guess you wouldn't lend me the car for the weekend, would you?"

"What do you want it for?"

"Just yes or no, Daddy, alright?" She takes the CAA book, and leafs through the map-pages.

"I couldn't do that, Terry. There's the shopping to do tomorrow, and Church on Sunday morning — "

"You could use a cab, couldn't you?" But she's given up. She finds Hartley in the index, turns to the page.

"Be reasonable," he says. "Besides, Mummy might like to go for a drive."

Terry butts out her cigarette in the ashtray. It's been cleaned out already. "Well I want to go to my Mother's funeral," she says.

"I'm sorry," he says. "Oh, dear."

"Skip it," she says. Hartley's not far from Lupton, she was through there once. "I just want to get away for a few days, that's all."

"Same old Terry," he smiles, but unhappily. "Always, out of the blue, some impractical impulse. Mummy used to worry, you know, that you might be a little — unbalanced."

"Oh, jesus."

"I always took your side on that point, Terry."

Daddy's face always came round doorways like a turtle's, expecting the worst. "Were you worried I'd turn out like her?" Terry slaps the book shut.

"We didn't know her, Terry. We only heard from her once."

"When was that?"

He sighs, nervously starts the engine. "She sent something, when you were seven."

"What?"

"A card," he says, "and a little dress. It was absurd really — frilly, nylon, hideous. And far too small for you."

"But you didn't give them to me."

His face wants to run and hide. He drives carefully out into the traffic, and stops at the next intersection, on a yellow light.

"You could have got through before it changed."

"Oh, Terry."

"So what colour was it? The dress."

"I don't remember, Terry — white I suppose."

"And what did you do with it?"

"It was so long ago. I imagine it went to the Salvation Army." And, as he drives off again, before she can start in, "We wrote your mother and told her it would be best for everyone if she didn't contact you. It's not as if she'd shown any interest for the first six years of your life." He only ever spoke forcefully when he was quoting Mummy.

"She may have changed or — seen things differently."

"Mummy and I had to think of you."

"This'll do," she says, as they cross 12th Avenue. "Right here," and has the door open before he's stopped. She gives him the hug that she thinks was meant for Tony and he murmurs in embarrassment.

"Bye," she says, and runs back and across the street as the lights change.

The meridan trees arch over 12th, it's the prettiest vista in the city in summer, but the houses are faded after the first two blocks, some derelict and slumping, waiting for apartment developers or for the middle-class to redeem them. The only garden intact for the last block is at the De-Tox house. A group of men lounge on the stoop there; a native youth, about her age, adjusts the lawn sprinkler. She's been noticing pregnant women, now she's noticing natives. She remembers Daddy rolling on the lawn with her, under the sprinkler jets. She strides across the parking lot, patting René's grey Saab as she passes.

Carla's at the desk: "Hi, René told me. How is she?"

"She was gone," Terry says. "Hell, I'd never met her — forget it . . . René busy?"

"I'll call him," Carla turns to the console. "No, it's only some voice-over shit — go on through."

In the viewing room a crumpled actor with a young voice talks into a mike as he watches the screen. Underwater shots of coral, then a boat full of beautiful people off a beach. A girl surfaces in a snorkel mask.

"You hear your own breathing, and the beat of your flippers, and at the same time you can listen to the cicadas and the parrots in the palms on the shore just above you.

You are between worlds. And beneath you stretches the paradise garden of the reef, ablaze with its living jewels, the fish — "

"We'll try it," a woman calls. Ann Friessen. "Thanks, David." The lights come up. "What d'you think, René?"

"It's okay." He stands up at the front, waves at Terry. "But for me, it would work better in a girl's voice . . . "

"Like 'Come on in' instead of 'This is the score'?"

"Yes, I guess so."

"Okay, we'll try that." Ann waves to Terry too. "Who've we got?"

"I do a marvellous Gidget," the actor pipes, falsetto. Everyone laughs.

René comes up to the door. "You alright, *poupée?* I said not to come to work."

"She was dead already. No big deal." They walk out to his office.

Terry takes a cigarette from the box on his desk. "She was native, René. Imagine that. I'm half-indian."

"Not so much of a surprise, *hein?*"

"No. I used to wonder . . . Doesn't bother you?"

He throws up his hands and leans on the desk beside her. Some of his mannerisms remind her of how much older he is, and how foreign.

"Eh, be real, kid. There's no old family in Québec without some Indian blood — what's the difference?"

Terry draws patterns in the ashtray with her match-stub. "So if you knocked me up and I had a brown baby — "

"Hiawatha Lauzon. Sounds great." Carla is at the door with a stack of magazines.

René gets up and twirls, turning the moment into a skit. "You are never boring, *ma poupée,*" he says, waltzing round the desk. "You could for sure make trouble for the wrong man."

"Sorry," Terry says. "I never said it."

Carla winks at René and dumps the magazines on the coffee table. It's never occurred to Terry that Carla has been there too.

"No problem," René laughs, "But now I have to announce to my colleagues that I have a vasectomy!"

"Vasectomies don't always take."

He leans back in his chair: "This one will!"

Carla raps twice on the wooden desk top and heads for the door. "Pray for rain," she says.

"Well?" says René.

"Can you lend me a car."

He checks her eyes: "You going somewhere?"

"I want to go to her funeral. She had a sexy husband."

"Oh, yes? When is it?"

"Saturday."

"So why don't I take you? You could feel out of place, or — "

"No, I want to get off anyway, think about some stuff. Can you lend me a car?"

"Sure," he shrugs. "You can have the Saab."

"You won't need it?"

"Not if you're out of town!"

"Won't your wife wonder? What'll you — "

"I told you. How many times must I tell you? At my age you don't waste time with small lies. No problem, okay?"

"Okay, great. Where's the keys?"

"You don't mess about, kid!" She still can't resist the fine lines at his eyes. She wants to lean over and run her hands inside his shirt, but she's in high gear. "Come on . . . please."

He digs out his key ring, and separates a smaller ring with two keys and the Capricorn medallion on it.

"Thanks." She mimes a kiss to him, grabs an Ovation mint from the bowl on the coffee table and goes out with it wedged in her lips like a cheroot. "Bye!" she calls.

"Drive careful, *poupée.*"

She walks past the empty front desk, tossing the keys up and catching them like the girl in his Jeep commercial.

She leaves the car running outside the apartment, stuffs a bag with a few days' things, takes all the beers from the fridge and puts them back in the carton, and runs out.

She takes the Lewvan to the ring road, swings north and then boots it to the highway.

She didn't even tell him where she was going. He didn't even ask.

What will he say when he knows that his child is growing inside her? If she tells him.

The fields of flax and canola are a chequerboard of mauve and yellow, wheeling away on both sides. Almost mesmeric. Now Rape is called Canola, Reserves are First Nations, UI is EI. O Canada.

She gulps at her beer and lodges the bottle between her thighs. The car is so quiet and luxurious. She plays with the air conditioning, the windows, the mirrors, the seat-adjustments — all the electronic buttons. This is slumming in reverse — do the rich feel this kind of pleasure when they check into a cheap motel?

She presses the tape which projects from the cassette deck. Keith Jarrett. Well, what the hell . . .

She takes me to be with herself.
Inside her, inside this moving room, across the wide land.

The sun wheels, the fields peel back,

I see through her eyes.

We pursue each other.

She rummages, in the pile of cassettes on the seat beside her. "Wish You Were Here", "Pat Garrett and Billy The Kid", Joan Armatrading, Van Morrison. She's looking for highway music. There's a kid's drawing mixed up with the cassettes — a man, a woman, a dog, a house, a spider-sun; green, yellow, red, and I LOVE YOU DAD, *JE T'AIME PAPA* filling most of the page.

What a rat's nest. She doesn't want to deal with that shit. She isn't over this morning yet, too much stuff going down all at once, and that shitty dream again, the terrified child, still lingering, doomy. Where the hell does it come from? — she can't be sure if she's always had it or if it's just the vague dread she used to wake up to, taking the form of a crying child. Maybe it goes with pregnancy, like the sickness that didn't come this morning.

She comes over the hill past the monastery, down towards Craven and the valley's edge. Hardly a vehicle on the glaring blacktop. She ejects the piano tape, picks out "Court and Spark" and slips it in, pressing fast-forward and band 3 on the display.

It's a wonder to her that René hasn't noticed the change in her boobs. She can't work out if the child crying in her dream is really young, or maybe twelve or thirteen, scared back into little-girlhood. Maybe it's something she's forgotten from her own childhood, a playback.

The stereo clicks, the green play light pulses. Okay.

She presses the button to tilt back her seat and then, as the song starts,

The mockery in Joni's voice as she swoops inside Coyote Man's head,
drinking alone, on the make in the Empire Hotel, about to cut loose,
or the music is anyway, guitars and piano calling the shots,

she adjusts the speaker buttons and the volume so
the tune jumps into life behind her. She floors the pedal,
lifts her chin, and sings out. She's flying . . .

with the schoolgirl chorus, chanting behind the come-on lines, the
crying shames, the good times, the laughs . . . "Raised on
Robbery", one for the road . . .

Her lovely grip tightens upon me.
Her heart beats over me.
She lifts me into her voice, we shall never be this happy again.
She is waking me into herself.
We are flying together.

Terry goes out along the valley's rim, above the marsh-
es and the first stretch of reservoir, handling the curves as
if she were in a racing machine. A silver and mother-of-
pearl rosary swings from the rear-view mirror, tilting at
every corner, a gift from his wife maybe? "She's got what
she wants," René always says. Terry's only seen her once,
at the party where she and René got together. Elegant,
smart, with her own friends. Would she believe he was
spending this time with a lab-assistant? Presumably she
wouldn't care.

But what the fuck's *she* going to do?

René's been right about so many things. But always the
insistence that she'd grow out of him, that he was there to
help, but the age difference was too much. Was he right
about that too? She used to object to *"ma poupée"* and
"kid"; now she accepts them, almost glad to be reminded.
And, hot though she is for him still, she *does* notice his
aging, his breathless moments, his intolerance of things
that still excite her — some of her music.

He's so cool, he laughed or ignored her out of all her games. He taught her things about love, and sex, and herself. It's not so simple, this growing out of someone. And the rotten timing of getting knocked up, half of her not wanting the abortion. And, fuck, he's her only real friend now.

She counts off the signals he's dropped for her:

"So you're not educated, *poupée*, you don't know much, but you're *smart.*"

"You can be tough, Terry, without having to be hard, *hein?*"

The time he said, "I admire you more than anyone I ever knew. You should admire yourself."

"I do admire myself," she'd said, and in that moment it had become true.

And she'd learned how to cry, with him.

Telling him, one time, some of the stuff she'd got into after she'd left home, the people she'd hung out with, and him saying, "You were a *touriste*, Terry, that's all, learning the score. I was the same.

"Just passing through and knowing it. Someone like you has *les anges gardiens, hein?* — *les bon anges* — guarding angels?"

His gifts to her, like the beads on the rosary in front of her. *Fuck.*

She puts the Van Morrison tape in: "Take it where you find it", "Lost dreams and found dreams in America". Will another lover ever mean to her what René means. Sometimes so gentle, sometimes unlocking screams from both of their throats. She remembers the cries from her parents' room. When she thought Daddy was beating Mummy up, which made no sense at all in the day to day world. Mummy's pale spite, no real malevolence, her tears when she wanted her way.

The vulgar white nylon dress, "Far too small for you," the birthday card, clumsy and illiterate no doubt as the message to René on the seat beside her.

Shiiiiiit!, she yells, banging the wheel, killing Van Morrison dead. This whole trip is pointless.

And then there's the sign: *Lupton. Hartley.* No mileages. What's she doing? This is just an excuse — she's not going there.

The car slows as she crosses the reservoir dam. The lake is twenty feet below the highwater stain. A couple of kids are walking across, lean pike or pickerel dangling from their hands, steaming in the sun. Native kids, naturally. There's a flock of geese circling overhead, as she climbs the west slope, twenty or thirty of them, tumbling as they reach the lake and then rising again.

The road turns north, through the scant sandhill pastures, and she pulls over at the first gate.

She sits for a few minutes with the engine off, till the heat gets too much, and her thighs start to stick to the seat. She takes a beer with her, climbs the gate and walks slowly till she's out of sight of the road, up the side of a small gully.

There are cactuses everywhere in the sparse grasses — chains of prostrate prickly-pears, and isolated, symmetrical pincushions. God, it's a marginal place.

But it's hot, and the geese are still flying and tumbling, and the sky is completely clear. She lies down by a gopher hole, the ochre sand-tailings; puts the beer aside, closes her eyes, and empties her mind.

> Between heaven and earth
> I unfold beneath her ribs
> I steal through her while she sleeps under
> the sky.

I came in her sleep, she sleeps for me, I sleep for myself
She breathes for me, until I can breathe for myself

She awakes to the sound of breathing. Standing in a circle around her are five bulls, heads down, only a few feet off. They are all different colours, they all have rings through their noses. She leaps up, screaming, waving her arms: "Fuck off! Get lost! Go on — scoot!" She's terrified.

Then she sees a man coming up the hill. "Easy!" he calls. "They won't hurt you."

He pushes between a white bull and a skewbald one. They snort and wheel around and come back. Their amazing, eggplant testicles. "They're only trouble if there's cows around," he says, and stoops to pick up her beer bottle, lying spilled by the gopher hole. "Can't have glass lying around," he says, without accusation. "Sun shines through it and next thing you know what little grass we have is up in smoke."

His eyes are blue as the sky. He wears a cowboy hat, boots with spurs and chaps. He's a movie hero, his teeth are white, he's gorgeous. And he hasn't looked at her tits once. "Hope I'm not trespassing," she says.

"That depends why you're here," he smiles.

"I was just taking a break from driving."

"Where you headed?"

"I was going to Hartley."

"Uh huh — I can point you out a shortcut."

All the bulls have curls on their brows, like the hair on René's chest, but silky. "Why do you keep the bulls together? Don't they fight?"

"Only if there were cows around, and we don't allow them that privilege. They're our breeding stock — Char'lais," he points to the white bull, "Simmental," the skewbald, "Limousine — what we call exotics."

"You mix them all up? Not purebreeds?"

"No," he says, and gestures her to follow him down the hill. "Purebreds are trouble, sooner or later. Mixing the breeds, if you get it right, gives you a better yield, a healthier herd. Hybrid vigour it's called." She watches the tapering back, the cute bum. The world is full of beautiful men! And this one has character — she sees most young guys as pin-ups.

"Which bull would win?" she asks, catching up with him. "If they did fight?"

"Well," he says. "I suppose the old Simmental — he's got 200 lbs on the others. But this is his last season. He's bologna come September."

"Bologna?"

"That's right," he shrugs, smiling lightly. She can hardly believe a man like this can be so gentle. "Bologna Bulls is what they're called. Just too old and tough even for ground beef."

Suddenly the lazy brute maleness back there seems pathetic. The curls on their brows. "Hey, that's not fair," she says, "just killing them off like that, after what they've done for you. And don't call me city folks, okay?"

He smiles broadly: "As you wish. But you have to be realistic — and they have a good life. A lot of folks would envy them."

She tells herself not to play female games here: "Do you always wear that getup?"

"It's practical," he says, and helps her over the gate. His hand is comfortable, touching a woman — strong but unassertive on her forearm. She makes sure their eyes know each other a moment.

"No gunbelt?"

"Wrong movie," as he swings over the gate. "I don't even hunt antelope."

The geese have swung round again; they come crying over them and tumble through the air with the ragged sound of washing on a windy line. "I've never known them flock up so early," he says. "They must know something we don't."

"Do you hunt *them?*"

He shakes his head: "No, ma'am, not that I've anything against it. But they've been around here longer than I have. Kind of gives a person faith in the Spring coming back." And laughs, with a first hint of self-consciousness.

His pickup is parked behind the Saab. "Nice car," he says. "Another exotic."

"Not mine. It's a friend's."

"Well," he hands her the empty bottle. "I'm Andy Mortensen. We're up at the first farm on the left. You come by again? — drop in. You'll be welcome."

"Okay, and thanks. My name's Terry. Dawson." And she gives him her hand. He's getting crowsfeet already. Character. "Thank you for saving me from the bulls."

"Like I said, they wouldn't hurt you. Only thing to worry about up there would be wood ticks."

"Oh!" she pulls a face. "Gross!"

"Yep, they even give me the creeps."

"Even you?"

His eyes enjoy the mockery. They slip down to check her hand for rings. He points up the road: "Take the second right," he says. "It's not much of a road but it'll save you a few miles. Maybe twenty minutes drive."

The pickup overtakes her as she reaches the turnoff. She returns his wave and honks twice. The road hasn't been graded all summer; she bottoms out after fifty yards and spends the rest of the drive zigzagging, to keep the wheels on the highest ridges of the gravel.

Her mind separates into its different levels, parallel but sometimes interwoven, like the parts in a music score. It's the thing about her René has never understood, why he so often asks, "Where are you, kid? *Qu'est ce que tu pense?*" And when she says, "Nothing," it's true, because it's never word-thoughts that he'd understand, or clear memories. He doesn't get her music anyway, the songs that are always the medium her consciousness works through. He only knows the music that she blasts from her stereo, or when they drive together, and then — even when he shares her taste — he tells her "Noise, noise, you kids are just scared of silence."

As part of her steers the low Saab over this obstacle course, another imagines Andy Mortensen submitting to her. Oh we give people something when we give them our names. He must be well into his twenties, but she knows that he's innocent next to her.

At the same time, the songs go on — Chrissie Hynde's voice belting it out inside her — and she realises that's twice today that a man from another world has said, "You'll be welcome." Yes, René's become her whole life; he still has his family, all of his friends intact, but her life's been narrowing down around him. Like when you're in love at fourteen and you dump your girlfriends for a boy . . .

"Don't get me wrong," the tough pleading voice wrong side of the tracks and sensitive as a whippet, counting out her faults as she gallops to sweet seduction . . .

She's only taking this road because Andy was following. The world's waiting,

René's right; he's always right. She's not going to stop at Hartley, she's not going to the goddamn funeral . . .

"Don't get me wrong," a nightingale with scars and a driving bassline, Thumbelina's mother, passionate, passionate screw-up, and rocking . . .

René won't know; she can have the abortion next weekend, and start living again . . . *How could any man resist that voice, that honesty? "Don't get me wrong" . . .*

Hartley begins as one street, but forks almost at once into three, with the right branch paved, and a store to the left with gas pumps by the road. She pulls in, gives the boy who comes out twenty bucks, and goes inside to get cigarettes.

A man is on a ladder, shelving cans that his wife passes up to him. "Where you from?" he says, and climbs down, ready to talk. Terry tells him "Regina" and pays for her smokes. She's fidgeting to get back on the road.

"You got any other kind of money?" the woman asks.

"Sorry?"

"People don't use two-dollar bills round here, unless they have to. And I won't get to the bank till Tuesday."

Terry fishes a crumpled ten bill from her jeans. "You're joking, right?"

The woman takes the bill. "Bad luck," she says. "Two-dollar bills come out in the Depression, people just don't like them."

"I always heard it different," the man says. "They're whore bills, if you'll excuse me, Miss — two bucks was the price of a whore back then, and that's how the bills got their bad name."

"You learn something every day." Terry pockets the change and strips the cellophane from her cigarettes.

And as she lights one at the doorway says, in spite of herself, "You wouldn't know anyone called Metcalfe here, would you?"

The man points across the road: "Name on the mail box," he says.

"We bought this store from Archie Metcalfe," the woman comes out to the door. "He's not a well man, you know — sister come out from England, after his wife died, takes care of him. You connected?"

"On my mother's side, yes. Thought I might look in on them."

The boy is peering in at the Saab's dashboard. "I wouldn't drive up their driveway," he tells her. "It's the pits."

"No, leave it here," the man says.

"Okay, I won't be long. Did you know their daughter?"

"Didn't hear of one," the woman says, "but we only came here five years ago. Or maybe there was a girl, was there, Len — got into trouble or something?"

"Something like that." The man looks over his glasses at Terry.

The woman's eyes kindle with interest: "Is that your connection?"

"You got it," says Terry. "I guess I was the trouble." And heads off past the car. "You can move it over for me, can't you?" she winks at the boy. "You bet!" he says and spits, macho, into the dust.

The driveway starts with a mass of lilac bushes, then goes to the left past a dried-up lawn and a jungle of a garden, with a small patch of corn and chrysanthemums and climbing beans. The house is two-storied, weather-bleached and with one porch-gutter down, but it's solid. There's a big shed twenty feet out on the north side, with a rusty weathervane, a rooster, above the door. Even in this heat there's a shimmer of smoke above the house's brick chimney stack.

Terry stands by the porch. A woman comes round from the south side, arms full of washing, and hesitates, staring in astonishment. "Can I help you?"

"Hi. My name's Terry. I believe my mother grew up in this house."

The woman has a long face, she's about sixty, she has nervous green eyes. "Oh, I don't think so, dear. This house has been in our family for forty two years."

"Maria. Maria Metcalfe?"

"Oh . . . " the woman stares dreadfully. "Then you . . . " Her neck flushes.

"I'm her daughter."

"Oh. Well, of course, I didn't know her . . . " The words come out at a rush, the woman seems stranded, stuck with the pile of sheets against her chest. She looks up at the porch, and then back to Terry. "The truth is, my brother's never talked about that. But come on in," she says, "we hardly ever get visitors," and fairly runs up the steps, dumping her laundry onto a wooden bench there. "Come on in, come on. We'll have a cup of tea." And as Terry hesitantly moves: "And don't you mind him — he's had three strokes now and, you know . . . It was Terry, wasn't it? Yes. Did you keep the name?"

"Terry Dawson."

"Dawson, oh. Well, that's an English name too, isn't it?" Some of her agitation is taken up by her hands. They are long and much abused by detergents. A thick wedding band on her right middle finger. "My brother can be cross," she says, with some defiance.

"Look, I didn't come to cause any trouble for you — "

"No, no, I'm glad of the company. Truly I am. And Archie hardly notices people, or the things that are done for him." There's bitterness too. "My name's Janet. Metcalfe too, of course — I never married."

> I am the stone under her heart.
>
> She clenches herself against me, but I will not let go.
>
> The ripples have stopped, the stone is frozen.
>
> She must take in this air, I have no need for it. I will sleep and be still.
>
> Her life will warm the stone, it will start to beat, in spite of her, in spite of this place.
>
> The ripples will go out again, before they close in.
>
> She will know me soon. Soon she will give me my life.

The television is blaring. The room smells of bread, and disinfectant and wax polish. The man sits in an upright chair, in pajamas, a thick cardigan, with a plaid blanket over his knees, beside the oil cookstove.

His hands are pale as death, wasted versions of his sister's. He doesn't look up, his chin has a constant tremor through it.

"You just sit down on the couch," the woman fills a kettle at a sink through the side door. She does everything at a run, talking the whole time, while the TV blares on, *The Young And The Restless*, and the old man ignores them both.

Janet Metcalfe brings a milk jug and sugar bowl to the table at the room's centre. Chattering about the problems with oil stoves, all the things she had to get used to when she came out to Canada, the weather. The room is spotless but faded and bare. It has the air of having been half-cleared out — perhaps to make room for the invalid. Pictures of English stately homes and landscapes, a Dutch pendulum clock in the open stairwell. Flowered wallpaper and brown trim. A varnished plank ceiling. Terry can't see any photographs.

"Archie," Janet calls, standing by his chair. "Do pay attention and say hello to Miss Dawson."

His face twists in irritation; he stares round till he fixes on Terry. His eyes are a similar green to his sister's, but drained and watering. His jaw-tremor is more pronounced face on, shaking his lower lip. "Who's this?" he demands.

"Miss Dawson," says Janet patiently, at the top of her voice. "Terry Dawson. She is . . . ," she hesitates. "Terry is the girl's daughter, Archie — she's come to see the house."

"My mother's dead," Terry says. "She died this morning, or last night. I never met her."

"Eh?" the man quavers. His left hand makes little waving motions above the chair arm.

"Maria's daughter, Archie. Maria has passed away."

Terry stares at his face. He seems to be looking through her. Some girl on the TV says "Harold hasn't been home since Tuesday night. I'm out of my mind with worry."

"She was no good!" says the old man. He grips the chair arms and turns himself back to the set. Terry looks up at Janet. "He wouldn't do this," says the TV, "unless something was terribly wrong." The old jaw trembles, a line of saliva runs out at the corner of the mouth. Janet dabs at his mouth with a paper towel. "You mustn't mind him," she says, "he doesn't know what he's saying." "No good," the man mumbles, "no good." "Oh Archie," Janet shouts, "be reasonable." "I'm sorry," says a black TV voice, "but your husband has AIDS."

Terry gets up. "I'm going," she says. "I have to get back to town." But Janet has the kettle off the stove and is over by the door at once. "No," she cries, "you mustn't. Not just yet. Let's go for a walk together."

"A walk?"

"Would you like to see your grandmother's grave?" The eyes are desperate with appeal.

"Okay."

They go by a trail through the field out back. "It's heartbreaking for Archie to see the place run down so, but there's only so much I can do." Janet talks on, as if frightened that any silence would find her alone again. "I'm afraid it keeps him even more within doors. He has a wheelchair, but he's never used it since I came. He doesn't like to go out on the verandah even, except some hot nights, after dark."

Terry talks, just to stop the exhausting chatter. "It must have been hard for you, coming out when you did."

"Well he needed me, dear. And our mother had died just a few months before. I looked after her," she says, with a conscious dignity, "for twenty-three years."

"That's awful." Terry stops and turns to her: "You've had no life of your own."

The woman smiles, gratified. "Oh, we mustn't grumble," she says.

"I'd grumble," says Terry. "I'd scream blue murder and tell them where to get off!"

The woman's both pleased and disapproving. They walk on in silence for a couple of minutes, down a lane past the schoolhouse.

The cemetery is small, with two big fir trees at the centre and a carragana hedge all around. There are grasshoppers everywhere among the stones. "We haven't kept things up too well, I'm afraid," Janet says, "but I get a boy to clear the weeds once a month." She points to the stone and stands tactfully back, though she cannot bring herself to leave altogether.

It's polished granite. *To the Memory of Theresa Tekwaysis,* it reads, *Beloved wife of Archibald Metcalfe, 1931–1984.* There is room for his name underneath. Theresa. "Was she his daughter?" Terry asks. "My mother?"

"Oh no, dear." Janet comes close, too close, and looks down at the stone. "No Archibald took her in, and the little one. He was a kind man."

She slips her arm through Terry's. She has the old woman smell of some harsh talcum powder. "Oh, if you'd seen him when he was young," she says, tears starting in her eyes. "We all idolised him. He was the eldest, you see, and the rest of us were girls. And then he went off to Canada, and sent us cards and presents, and then came the war and he was wounded, and we hardly heard from him till his health started failing." She plucks Terry's arm: "Come on back," she says. "I mustn't leave him too long." And then with a gust of sentimental passion: "He deserved better from life than this."

"It must be lonely for you," Terry says, and detaches her arm as they move off. The woman stands for a moment, indulged in the grief that she's raised in herself. There is pain and pride and defiance, all muddled up as "Stay!" she cries, her hand flying out grotesquely, "stay for the night. It *is* lonely. Please say you'll stay." And then hurries up, and says slyly, "You could sleep in your mother's bed."

They eat at the central table, though Archie's chair is turned so he can watch the TV. *Dallas.* Janet sits close beside him, and cuts his food, helps some of it into his mouth, wipes his chin. He ignores Terry, but his sister keeps talking through the TV noise, and scarcely touches her own food. But there's a bottle of gin, and some tonic. Janet encourages Terry to drink, and matches her.

Halfway through the meal Archie lets out a long, burbling fart, and Janet supports him out through the door by the stairwell. God, Terry thinks, never, never, *never*. It's like one of René's self-mocking scenarios when she first talked about love.

They come back in to the table, Archie oblivious to his sister's exertions, her shaking hands once he's slipped back into his chair. "You know nothing about Dieppe!" he says, glaring at Terry. "Nothing at all." His hand comes up and taps uncontrollably on the table.

"Oh, don't start," Janet begs. "He'll ruin his dinner."

"Harry Riddell," he says, his eyes accusing, "Harry Riddell. The best friend a man ever had. Harry Riddell." He leans forward at Terry, Janet pulls his plate away from his sleeve. "We got up the beach," he says, his eyes boring into her, "up safe by the sandcliffs, half the regiment dead on the beach behind us. 'We're safe,' I said. And Harry said to me, right there he said:

'Oh little did my mother think,
The day she cradled me
That I'd be stormed by shot and shell
To —'

and this shell came in, and he stopped that poem, because his head was blown off. Right then, right beside me."

His jaw trembles, his eyes spring up with tears, there's a terrible wounded beseechfulness about him. Terry reaches over and puts her hand over his. It is dry and cold. "She was no good!" he says, and turns back to *Dallas*.

They have a couple of drinks after Janet puts him to bed, but Terry's energy nosedives. "I've got to sleep," she says. "It's been a crazy day."

Janet is too slewed to protest much. "I've put a hot water bottle and fresh sheets on," she says, as if skirting a tongue twister. "You go on up, I've more chores to do."

"You should get some sleep too."

"No, I don't need much." She pours the last of the gin into her glass.

"Goodnight Janet."

"Goodnight dear."

Archie's bed is downstairs, in the old living room. Janet has the main bedroom next to the upstairs bathroom: it's an old fashioned child's room — pink everywhere, flounces around the bedstead, a clutter of ornaments, dolls and photographs. And the smell of that powder she wears.

Terry's room is littered with cardboard boxes, full of preserving jars and gin bottles. Bare plaster walls. The window looks out on the shed, and the weathervane. An empty closet, a bare lightbulb, a narrow bed. But it is warm and soft, though the smell of the hot water bottle is like condoms, and she kicks it out onto the floor.

Gin and exhaustion. She has no time to think about this, her mother's room and bed, to think anything. She curls up on her side, naked, with her hands between her knees, and sleeps.

I cry. I am the crying she hears, the child weeping inside her dream. I am crying and will not stop. She struggles to escape into the light. My tears are embedded in her own moaning. She is desperate to come awake.

She knows me. She has heard me before.

She's awake. Something fell over. She can hear arguing in the next room. A man's voice rises to a shout, a woman's wailing, there's an exclamation, a smacking blow, and someone staggers against furniture.

"No-ohh," she hears the woman's voice.

Then a door dragged open.

"No!" the voice is clear now. "No, you mustn't!" Tears and pain in the cry. "Please come back!"

It's too dark to see anything. Foreboding trembles up through her. She stretches up for the light cord, has to kneel up to reach it. There's stumbling on the landing, a man's raging, "Get back, woman — get back to bed!"

Her bedroom door opens softly. There's a man there, looking at her. He wears a blue dressing gown. He gestures violently as a woman grabs at his left arm.

"Get off! he shouts. His voice is flat, and echoes in the room. Terry feels the hopeless sobs beginning in her stomach. She can see the woman, short and dark, in a white nylon nightdress, her hair wild. "Don't!" she cries, tugging again at the man's arm. "You promised! Please, honey, come back to bed!"

The top of the man's dressing gown is pulled open. He twists to free himself and his other arm goes up. The sound of the blow is like firewood splitting. The woman falls out of sight. He comes in and closes the door.

She crosses her hands over her chest. The whimpering is trapped in her throat. She sits by her pillow, unable to move. Down the centre of his chest is a scar like a zipper, grey.

He stares at her. She cannot stop the whimpering. She reaches up and pulls the light-cord.

The ripples go out.

We possess each other.

The crying stops. Terry's awake again. She sits bolt upright, and tears the wet bedsheets away from herself.

Her heart is panicking, her tongue is numb — she was biting it.

"Shit!" She flings her legs out of bed and stands, unsteady. She threads her way through the litter of boxes and bottles, and drags the window up. It falls back with a crash. She gets one of the bottles and props it open.

There's already some light in the sky. The air is dry and still warm, there's the smell of wolf willow. Everything is still.

She looks directly out at the weathervane on the shed roof. As her mother must have looked out at it. Her hands go up to her swollen nipples. "Sweet jesus," she tells the night.

She goes back and sits on the bed. Do they lock the house? She'll never get back to sleep now. Her heart is still racketing. She lies back again in the half-dark, her hands behind her head.

Then Janet is at the door. "Terry, I brought you some coffee." Her eyes avert from the girl's nakedness. "It's ten o'clock, dear. Did you sleep well?"

When Terry comes down, he's by the stove again, but the TV's still off. "I'm really late," she tells Janet. "I have to leave right away."

"You'll come back and visit?" The long face is grey and pathetic.

"Maybe," says Terry. "Anyway, thanks for the hospitality."

"It's a joy," Janet says. "It's a joy to have visitors."

The old man has not looked up. He stares at the blank TV, jaw trembling, hands loose and white on the chair arms. There's a streak of spittle on his cheek, Janet reaches for a paper towel. "No let me." Terry takes the towel and dabs at his face, the spittle hangs over the sparse white bristles.

"You are a dear," Janet says. "Will you say goodbye, Archie?"

Terry gets hold of his pajama lapels, and pulls him straighter in the chair. He is almost weightless. She looks into the faded eyes, and tugs him a little closer. There's a flicker of fear there. She pulls the lapels wider, a button comes away. Just enough to see the top of the scar, a grey zipper pattern on the loose flesh of his chest. She releases him. "Goodbye, Father," she says quietly. The eyes stare drearily into hers.

At the end of the dead lawn she turns and sees Janet on the porch, bent over and peering out at her through the sunlight. It's roasting hot already. Terry waves. Janet doesn't seem able to see her.

The keys are still in the car. She drives off without looking in at the store. "Son of a bitch," she says to herself, "son of a bitch, son of a bitch."

The beer is warm, but she opens one anyway, drinks, and lights a cigarette. "Alright, kid," she says to herself. "I know the rules. This is my last pack."

She pushes the tape in the cassette. Van the Man still, moaning and saying "yeah" and "alright" over some fiddle and guitar track. A voice out of René's world.

"But listen," she says, settling the bottle between her thighs, "One hour after you're born, one damn hour, I'm lighting up again. Okay?"

She's out of town, following a sign for Fort Qu'Appelle. The beer is sticky on her lips. She cranks up the sound; the speakers jounce by the back seat:

He's sauntering down the avenue, halfway between vaudeville and talking blues, offering second chances, so sure of himself, "The Healing Has Begun" . . .

A piano joins in with the tune, lifting the tempo.

"We're in this together, kid," she says, and picks up speed towards the valley. "You just better be a girl!"

Saturday, 12:25 and he sees the dust cloud coming fast down Highway 22. He backs the cruiser off the highway, and waits.

The car doesn't see him till it rounds the bend, 200 yards back. In his mirror he sees the driver reach quickly sideways and down. The car slows as it approaches. A woman, no passengers.

He turns on the roof-lights, puts on his hat, and steps out.

The grey Saab pulls up behind the cruiser. The girl has black hair to her shoulders, dyed on one side with a peacock-blue flash, a full, pretty mouth. "Any problem?" she says. There's a sassy look about her.

"Just checking, Miss," he says. He eyes the Miller case on the seat beside her. "Would you mind turning the music down, Miss?" Grasshoppers are banging into his boots and pinging off the car, masses of them out of the dry roadside grasses, like soft green bullets.

"You wouldn't have any open liquor in there, would you?"

The girl takes off her shades and grins up at him. Her eyes are a striking pale green, she's a beauty. She shakes her head. Her purse is on the floor by the passenger seat; he can see the beer stain spreading through it.

"May I see your licence?"

She reaches down, registers the spill, tries to dig out her wallet without exposing the bottle.

"Come on, Lady," he says. "You don't want to ruin everything in your purse. Bring it out."

She shrugs resignedly, hands him out the wallet and sneaks a last sip from the bottle before he takes it from her and empties the dregs on the road.

She dodges a grasshopper and rolls up her window. He walks round, checking the car over, and motions her to unlock the passenger door. When he's halfway back to the cruiser with the beer case, she calls out. "What do you do with the stuff?"

He opens the trunk. "We dispose of it."

"Yeah, I bet!" She's standing by her car.

"That's what they all say. It's like a record." He slams the trunk. "Now, would you bring your registration, and come to my car?"

He calls in her licence number. No record. She gets in beside him and picks up his hat from the seat.

"Who is René Lauzon?"

"A friend." She twirls the hat on her finger. Her perfume is delicate, classy.

"Does he know you're out here?"

"Look, Buffalo Man," she says. "I'm not a car thief. Of course he knows."

He reaches for his hat. "Buffalo man?"

She twirls the cap, out of his reach, and points to the RCMP badge. Her eyes dare him to relax. She's cute, alright, and she's not wasting time getting mad at him.

"What'll it cost me?" she asks, and she puts his hat on, and moves his rearview mirror to admire herself in it. She tucks her hair back behind her ears: "Do you think they'd have me?"

"In the Force?

"Sure — I can ride a horse."

He laughs. "It wouldn't hurt our image," he says. "The ticket's for fifty dollars if you pay on time."

"Can I keep just one of the beers?"

"Are you serious? Now just give me my hat."

"Hey, I'm going to a funeral. Got to keep my spirits up."

"Where's the funeral?"

"Lebret. My mother."

"I'm sorry," he says. He looks at her curiously: "I wouldn't have took you for a native." Though with those cheekbones, the hair — only the eyes don't fit.

"I didn't know I was, till yesterday."

"That the truth?"

"Mm-hmm. She asked for me just before she died. Weird eh?"

He hands her back the papers. "You can sign on the back of this, Teresa, if you want to plead guilty."

"It's Terry."

"Alright. Or you can contest it, on the date shown — there."

"Can I keep a beer?" Her eyes tease, but they don't put him on the spot.

"I'm not looking," he says. She touches his shoulder and grins again. She has wonderful, even teeth. He looks out the window; she has the grace not to let the bottle clink.

"Thanks, Buffalo Man," she says, and gets out.

She walks with a sort of lifting step. Happy. She's sexy as hell in her white cotton pants.

"Hey!" he leaps out of the car, all his police paranoia back in place. "You come right back here, right now!" His hand even feints towards his holster.

She has her car door open. She waves his hat at him: "I'm not stealing it," she yells. "Honest, I'll be right back."

She reaches into the Saab, squats down on the road and then stands, slamming the door. She comes back towards him. He gets back in.

She comes to the passenger door. "Sorry," she smiles. Her shades are back on. "Just wanted to get a rise out of you. I like you, Buffalo Man."

"Alright," he says. "Just give me my hat."

She sets it down carefully on the seat.

"Maybe see you again," he says.

"Not in the line of business, I hope. Yeah, well you never know. Bye."

He says, "Watch how you drive, Terry," as she slams the door.

The Saab drives past. She smiles and waves. He nods.

A nice encounter, he thinks. There's still a trace of her perfume in the cruiser. He picks up the hat. Three grasshoppers fly out of it into his face.

He swats them out the window, and leans back in his seat.

He sits for a while, listening to the hopper bombardment of the cruiser, watching her dust.

The Saab crosses the highway and heads straight for Qu'Appelle. But then he sees the dust settle near Number 10. After a minute, it starts up again, veering to the right, picking up speed along the valley side.

Well, the little cow, he thinks. Wherever she's going, it sure as hell isn't to Lebret.

ϓ ϓ ϓ

prelude

A few years ago a scientist was appealing on the radio for people to collect air from the attics of old Ontario houses. Preserved there, he said, would be the air that their grandparents breathed, which it would be useful to compare with the stuff that we breathe today.

I don't know whether it's "good science" to suppose that a glass ball, blown by someone long in the past, still contains his breath. Something of him clings to it anyway, as the touch of makers and owners clings to many artefacts. "Things men have made and breathed soft life into," in D.H. Lawrence's words, though in this case the life is not soft at all, but the fierce, arrogant, despairing testament of an artist.

Glass "fishing floats" from Japan used to be one of the prime beachcombing treasures on the North West Coast. Catalogues were published, identifying maker's hallmarks and age. Most of the floats were relatively modern, machine made, boringly perfect; but occasionally a small, dark sphere would turn up, with that touch of crudity that goes with the handmade. Some had been thrown up by storms, above the driftwood line, and had lain in the forest mosses for longer than they'd been on the ocean, but others were crusted with barnacles and may have wandered, as the float in this story does, almost endlessly on "the unplumbed, salt, estranging sea."

It was impossible to pick up such a treasure without wondering — as I would about an ancient harpoon point or arrowhead or coin — about its history, both human and elemental, and about the hands that made it, or the last hand to touch it. In a way, the finder of those treasures is making a human contact: touching another hand across the years. There's a language of sorts being spoken, unimpeded by time or space or mortality. The feeling involved is a rare kind of tenderness.

I feel that way about the float in this story. It's an image of isolation, I guess, but of endurance too. The tiny glass world is touched by four cultures — two of them "defeated", two "victorious" — before the old Korean's breath is released, and perhaps . . . but I shouldn't try to interpret my own story; the ending is enigmatic and should remain so.

THE GLASS SPHERE

The glass sphere had drifted on the Pacific for almost two hundred years. It had gone so far south that the ground swell of the Hawaiis had drawn it in, but then a southwester drove it back to the open sea and it went with the currents, northwest, riding high on the surface, entering wave troughs and skimming the swells and rollers, light as a seabird.

The birds had ridden it, too. Gulls, terns, and once — a thousand miles from land — an exhausted storm petrel, one of those brown life-sparks which American whalers called Mother Carey's chickens and believed were the souls of drowned seamen.

For years at a time it had been host to barnacles; their miniature atolls of lime had altered its balance, so that the boss of its closure had lifted clear of the water and it had spun anti-clockwise. The barnacle colonies came and went; they left crusts on the glass like faint, cryptic lettering U's, C's, and O's.

It had ridden the verge of a warm current, a wide ocean road for migrating fish and aimless flotsam like itself. It had bobbed past a bleached wooden boat where a stiff hand dangled and brushed against it, and dead eyes stared from the gunwales into its mirroring skin.

The light of the sun, moon and stars shone milky-green through it. In a kelp-raft below Alaska it had been for a season the plaything of sea otters, lounging in seaweed hammocks as they preened and suckled.

And for nearly two years it was beached up in the Aleutians, nudged further by every tide up a thin shell beach to a cleft in the basalt cliffs. The sun and salt had lustred its flanks with irridescent streaks. One dawn the sea crept in utter silence to the top of the island, carrying the glass sphere up through the trees, and then it withdrew in a fury, tearing the forest down with it, and for half the day a nest of young eagles had floated behind the sphere, till the nest disintegrated.

The sphere had frozen, and baked. The air inside it, which was the breath of a man, had made frost-flowers upon its walls, and had filled it with mist.

At the start it had been one in a chain, buoying a net between rudderless fishing junks, caught in a squall with a full catch. One boat had had time to cut itself loose, and had watched its partner dragged by the weight of the net into the wind's face and under the waves.

The boat fell slowly, the net pluming up behind it, into the stillness a furlong below the storm, leaving the colours of red, orange, yellow, suspended in that blue silence by the mass of dead fish and the glass spheres, and by the body of one of the sailors which had floated up into the net.

They hung there, lifting and sinking for almost a month, till the great grey fishes came, tearing into the swollen net. One of them got itself trapped and its death struggles ripped a whole skein of the net free. The catch floated back to the surface, the weight of the dead shark joined that of the boat and they slipped together, with the ruin of the seine, faster away from the light. A last strand of the net broke free, and the sphere that was bound to it flew to the surface, the pressure slackening inside it like the lungs of a desperate swimmer. It floated again, under a cloudless sky, trailing a rag of meshes.

The shawl of netting became a world, sustained by the glass sphere. Algae, then weeds, then molluscs and fingerling fishes lived wholly within its shadow, feeding each other and multiplying, suspending their eggs and shells from the weakening fibres. Beside and below moved the golden-eyed, watchful predators. The sphere lay heavier in the water, dragged at by colder currents, immune now to the shifts of the wind, till the netting rotted and that world fell away to extinction. The sphere rode high again, skating before the winds.

An infinitesimal orb on the ocean's face, it was almost inviolate. Minute abrasions, small shifts in refraction and texture, a milkier light. In the law book of western physics the sphere is as much a liquid as the sea that it drifts upon. In that book the windows of Chartres and York are in flux, they pour like still waterfalls between their frames, through the centuries, achieving such magical shades and harmonies as their makers could not have imagined.

But whether the sphere's creator would have accepted, or understood, the rules of our science is unknown. His touchstone was an obsidian blade, washed out from the bank of the Yalu; its formal design and refractive perfection were a message and consolation to him from the first glass-breeders. He was master of his craft but to him glass was nature transformed and restated, and the art was in permanence, not change. His physics, and chemistry, were the suspension of Time, and to harness that science and matter to a thing like a fishing-float was for him, degradation.

He lived in the prison of exile. The barbarians had come, as they'd come in each generation since his great grandfather's father, the atelier's founder, had watched Hideyoshi's armada in rout off Pusan. In the third year of his own mastery, he saw the atelier burned and the village with it. Saw the nose and ears of his Lord paraded down to the shore on a leather cushion, and was chained himself, with the porcelain makers, the ivory-carvers and jewellers, in the hold of a ship and brought to the land of borrowed manners and clothes, a bastard language, unspeakable food. Here where they worshipped power and ghosts, he was put to work.

The noble Satsuma who owned him was in debt to a merchant. The glassmaster went with a daughter, as part of her dowry, to discharge the debt.

His dreams were a vacuum; his grandfather's hands appeared to him no more. From dawn till the last watch he walked among labourers, debt-slaves with minimum talent, overseeing the vats of cheap, molten glass, trying to teach consistency in a place where the glass was blown into moulds. His life was an insult, but unlike the barbarians he feared his own death.

He dreamed, but they were empty daydreams. His son might be living yet, his owner might be persuaded in time to open a fine-glass workshop. He was aging and broken in spirit. He wondered sometimes if he had forgotten — if six generations of craft and judgement had died in him while he still lived.

The merchant cared only for property, and the growth of his fishing fleet, but he had no pretensions and he honoured success. He was shrewd, too, and guessed at the glass-master's anguish. Trade for the moment had over-ridden hostilities with Korea; he made enquiries.

One evening in March, when the larch buds were scarlet and the wolfbane had turned the headlands yellow, the merchant's son called the old foreman to his office. He held out a letter. It came from the master's wife, in the hand of a scribe for the women of his class pretended illiteracy. The young man watched as he read, and saw nothing. The glass-master bowed slightly, thanked him, and returned to the foundry.

His son and his grandson were dead. He breathed in the stench of the place, the coals and the schist-tainted glass, the sweat and the rice wine; for a moment, by the young merchant's window, he had smelled the Spring.

He snatched the blowpipe from the hands of the laborer nearest him and twirled its end through the surface of the vat. He took a great breath; all that was in his heart at that moment was grief and rage; he blew through the iron pipe.

Some of the laborers there would deny what they'd seen; others, in time, embroidered the truth. The man who had yielded the blowpipe would never forget, though. The old Korean had blown out a perfect float, without need of a mould, had walked down the gangway and plunged the sphere into the whale-oil vat, had fished it out with his hand and, after holding it up to his face, had thrown it down. It had not broken. He had come back and returned the pipe, without taking his eyes off the door at the end of the warehouse, and had gone out into the street. He was not seen again.

He did not die, though his mind might be said to have died. He disappeared into the floating world of Kagoshima.

His breath went out and survived him, drifting through space he could not have imagined, in its prison of glass. Five generations after his abdication it lay in a cul-de-sac of the ocean, passed back and forth by the currents from Japan and California, skirting the islands of Canada, outlasting the changing jetsam of the times.

In the month of July, a mile out of Naden Harbour, a girl's hands reached down from the stem of a fish boat and lifted the glass sphere from the water. The sea dripped back from it over her wrists, her face was curved and distorted in it, it was flushed through by the red sky in the west.

The boat moved on round the headland and drifted into the bay with its engines cut. "You should see this place," the fisherman said. "I like to stop in on my way home. My grandad was born here." He was an old man himself, though wonderfully active. He might have grown heavy in his middle years, but now he'd shrunk back to something like the muscularity of his youth. The boat ran gently onto the low-tide sand. He threw out a mud-anchor and they climbed into knee-deep water. He drew breath, his elbow on the gunwale. "It's called *K'ung*," he said. "*K'ung* means Moon in our language." He chuckled, and hauled a sack over the side: "It means knife, too. Who knows?" The girl reached for the blankets and clutched them to her chest. They waded ashore.

All she could see were the tumbles of moss-cloaked logs among the spruce trees, and two bleached houseposts, with animal-human faces, sagging above the sand. There was a fire-blackened ring of stones below a projecting

branch, and a stack of wood at the tree's base. She threw
down the blankets and stretched. "Its so good to be back
on land," she cried, "out in the open." She jogged on the
spot for a moment, shaking her wrists out loosely "And
this," she said, twirling around, "god, this must be the
most peaceful spot on earth!"

The fisherman squatted by the stone ring, building a
tent of kindling from his sack. "A lot of people died here,"
he said. He was matter-of-fact; there was no reproof. She
came and stood over him: "After we came, the whites, you
mean?" He put a match to an old cigarette pack under the
sticks. "Uh-huh," he said, squinting against the smoke,
"Disease and all that, you know. It was Scarlet Fever mostly." As the fire licked upwards the light seemed to die
from the sky, and the trees closed in.

"Are they all buried here?" The sticks crackled, her
voice seemed hushed. Their shadows were flat against the
trees and the housepost faces, dancing up with the flames.

The man poured some water into his billy can. "Surely,"
he said, and grinned up at her: "There's skulls and bones
all over, best watch where you walk!" He gestured for her
to pass him some logs from the pile. "There's a gravestone
or two, as well, but they're Swedes."

"Swedes?""

"Hmm. There was a whaling station here, for thirty
years. After the people gave up on the village. We called
them Swedes but they come from Norway I believe. They
went home for the winter, I guess. Just made a little world
of their own here, never got around." He brushed his
hands on his thighs. "And so some of them died here."

It was not cold but she squatted and held out her hands
to the flames. "Don't matter to us," he said, with one of his

droll, teasing faces: "Us Haidas come back again a few times, I told you that. Everyone got his *hoonts.*"

"*His* hoonts? Only the men?"

He laughed to himself, a sort of benign, soft cackle. "Ohh, ladies too. We are a very advanced people!"

"But look," she said, "there's a light on the boat."

He turned and squinted down the beach: "Now what could that be?" he said. "Ohh, I reckon it's that fishing float of yours, catching our firelight."

She stirred up the fire, and watched the answering flare above the water. "It looks like an eye," she said. "Do you find a lot of them?" He nodded: "Used to be; not so much anymore. I guess those Japanese using plastic now. Those bleach jugs do the job just as good."

"I think I'll go for a swim" she said, and stood up. "Okay?"

"It's safe," he said. "I'll heat up some grog while you're out."

Out of sight down the shore she took off her clothes and waded in. The tide had come in a little; the boat was shifting on its chain. The glass ball at the stem winked up and down. The water felt silken and safe; she was aware of the sweat and fishgrease, the fumes of the cabin from two months at sea drifting away from her on the surface. She swam round behind the boat and clambered over the side, got a towel and a clean sweater from the cabin, and came back to shore on her back, kicking lazily through the shallows, keeping the cloth dry.

The smoke was blowing towards her as she came to the fire. He looked up at her, took in the long sweater, almost to her knees, and held out a cup. "Sit next to me, girlie," he said. She hesitated — in the nine weeks she'd crewed for him, for all the jokes she'd put up with from the guys on the packer's barge, he had never made a pass, or a suggestion, or even looked at her that way.

She sat beside him, towelling her legs, huddled in front of the fire like a child. The mug of hot rye and sugar was innocent as cocoa. "There were ten big houses," he said. "Dancing, feasts. And all of the food that we needed right here." The sweep of his hand embraced the whole bay behind her.

"It must have been paradise," she said.

"It was good, yes. But people died then, too; people was hurt. People is people," he said. His hand touched her knee and began to caress it in little strokes, just the fingertips. They moved down, lifting her calf muscle, came back over her knee. She looked down at the hand, dark upon her thigh. "Were you ever with a white woman?" she said.

"Ohh," he laughed quietly, and took back his hand. "I'll not talk such foolishness with a lady like you." Back on shore, and on the ice-barge, he spoke pretty much like the other fishermen, but here he'd slipped into the near monotone of the older natives, hypnotic and lisping between the tide-lap and the settling coals.

"A lady!" she laughed, awkward now.

"Sure, he said. "You are getting an education."

"Oh come on!" she said. He held up his hand: "Now don't act ashamed of that," he said. "That *would* be foolishness." The hand fell back upon her thigh.

He was very gentle. She leaned back on her elbows; her eyes were closed. His voice was as soft as his touches: "We didn't lose near as much as it looks. We keep going," he said. "The changes are part of us too."

And then, "You are a smart girl, a pretty girl" he said, and turned over and lay on his side. Out at sea he had lain, stretched out in his bunk, on his back, lightly snoring; now he curled in like a child, hands thrust between his knees, his breathing inaudible. Yet she realised, almost at once, that he was asleep. He could have had her, and he left her. She would remember all of her life what did not happen.

She finished her drink and reached for one of the blankets. She lay on her back for a while, while branches shifted and fell in the forest, the sea hushed towards them, the anchor chain rasped. There was a mockery somewhere, hidden from her, like the faces up on the houseposts she could no longer see.

He gave her a small slate carving he'd done on the boat. A bear with her two, human cubs. It sat on the shelf above her bed in the residence, with her other summer trophies. A vase full of eagle feathers, an orange and yellow agate, the green fishing float with its barnacle runes.

The day after registration her boyfriend got back from hockey camp. They could scarcely wait for each other. Down the hall co-eds were shrieking and a dozen competing musics boomed out at the afternoon. They tugged off their clothes, laughing, rolling upon the bed. They could scarcely wait.

She thought, in the moment before he entered her, that she'd keep the old fisherman to herself. She was starved of this; it was strangely flagrant, and private too, making love while people ran shouting past her door and danced on the grass outside.

Here it came at last. She was both in control and beyond it. She was running, backwards, up the mountain, the valley beside it rolled over upon her. "Oh jesus," she cried, and her left hand flew from her lover's shoulder. It struck the shelf over their heads, the vase teetered and fell. Eagle feathers came down in a sheaf on their faces.

The glass sphere rolled from the shelf and dropped, from the pillow to the floor. A quick, high note rang back from the walls. The glass sphere shattered. The girl gasped for breath.

♈ ♈ ♈

prelude

The image of a young boy dragged by a horse across a field haunted me for years before I wrote this story.

It's a common enough hazard of riding, and I'd seen one of my daughters have her share of spills and collisions, preserved it always seemed by an ironic guardian angel; but this particular image was given to me by her mother.

She's a junior school teacher in England, and she phoned me one night to say that a boy in her class had just been killed while riding. There's a lot of the parent in a good teacher, and the story's vividness was scored by her special sadness.

I'm not the kind of writer who ever thinks There's something I can use. I just took the sorrow, and the image, into myself and, as I say, was haunted by it.

Till one day, three years ago, I became that boy instead of watching him. Then this had to written. In fact it involves more than a single story. A cast of characters grew around the dead child.

A child's view of life is a sufficient mystery, however much we're convinced we remember. A child's view of death (I do not mean the heartbreaking courage of a sick child sparing its parents' terrors) is an utter secret. We can only guess. But we *have to* guess.

Some of you will know the parlour game —
attributed usually to Carl Jung — which supposedly
charts your private world:

You are asked to imagine, and describe, the
house you would most like to live in. When you
leave the house, you describe the walk that you
take.

Then comes a series of encounters — you are
asked to describe them, and your reactions: You
meet a bear. You find a cup. You come to a stream.
You find a key. You come to a door . . .

The house represents your self (and any trees
you envisioned stand for friends).

The walk is your life; the bear is trouble; the cup,
love; the stream, sex; the key, knowledge; and the
door, death.

We played the game with my daughter Hazel
when she was seven years old — not as an experi-
ment, but because she didn't want to be left out . . .

When she found her key, in the grass across the
stream, she insisted that there were two of them: a
heavy iron one, like a castle door's, with a tiny silver
one linked to its handle. I thought, as she spoke, of
Walter De La Mare's lovely child-poem, "The Keys
Of The Morning" — Death and the Maiden were
already there in the room with us.

When she came to her door, set into the trunk of
an old tree, she opened it with the iron key, and
inside was another door which her silver key
unlocked. She was in a passageway now, with a faint
light at the end of it through a third, open door.

She went towards it; she was carrying a kitten, she said. There was a little room there, with a bed and a candle burning beside it on a table. She lay down on the bed, with the kitten in her arms, and blew out the light.

Often it is the unguarded innocence of young children that brings tears into parents' eyes. But once in a while, it is their knowledge.

BOLT

Between the stirrup and the field they called his name. There was a flash of sky through the horse's legs, so close to his face, before his shoulder sang out at the hurt and his cheek, on the other side, slapped the hard grass and rang yellow lights through his eyes.

He was tumbling and turning, curled in on himself and trying to breathe, and his name spun into a wall around the sides of the jolting paddock — first the linden tree and the house roof in an island of sunlight and then, as his arms fell back against the earth, the stonepile and the gate into the woods and then, while his face juddered along the grass and clods flew around him, the long shadows shuttling up the hill — all blurring under the horse's belly into a green and black and yellow wall that was climbing the sky.

The earth was hollow beneath the runaway hooves. He was dragged on his shoulders now — he could see his boot in the stirrup that would not let go — but everything was becoming loose, and soft. The wall that had grown from his name was a long sigh, closing around him, the

colours were fading. He felt his back spring outwards —
he was almost as high as the saddle for a moment — and
then he was staring at Williwaw's front hoof, with its
bright new shoe, the ten square-headed nails hammered
in just last week, the two shoulder-nails that Chris Lamont
said did all the real work — *The clinch nail, The clench
nail* . . .

The clods were flying into the sky — *the clinch nail, the
clench nail* — heavy and feathered and black. His name
was closing around him again, he was turning and turning — behind his wide eyes he could see the worm gear of
his father's press beginning to move, a dim shadow — *the
clinch nail, the clench nail* — his father's hands must be
gripping the wheel, they would count together, it took
seven turns — *the clinch nail, the clench nail* — to bring the
rollers down onto the bed. The worm gear turned and
ran downwards, yet it never moved . . .

There were sounds like the school orchestra tuning up,
behind the wall and the shadowy worm gear. Something
was creaking, something was twanging.

And Daddy's eyes stared down through the wheel, pale
blue eyes that stared down at the bed but could not see
him. *The clinch nail, the clench nail.* Daddy's hands turned
as if he was steering a car, and a wide cold voice said
"ONE."

The body brush was moving in quick circles, along the
horse's flank with a sound like feet in dry grass, leaving
dark furrows on the sweat-drenched coat. The girl's hand
was pale, under the brush strap, and her face was pale
against the horse's shoulder. In the gloom of the box stall
he watched his sister's face as he never had before, and
saw how young she was, as though the six years between

them had galloped away, and more, and he had grown
older than her.

She worked towards the horse's rump, following the
grain of its coat with her strokes, dipping into the contrary whorl of hairs by its haunch. Her breath was held in
as she brushed, as if the one thing on her mind was to do
this job perfectly; but the air in the barn was charged with
madness, the edges of things seemed ready to crack. The
horse's eye rolled back at her as she worked down its
thigh; the nerves in its skin leaped away from the brush
and sent tremoring waves through its leg.

The smells in the barn were like parts in a music: they
wove and surfaced through each other, and flowed, and
broke apart. Williwaw's breath blended in with the hay
and manure, but his sweat cut into the air like his staring
eye and conjured the taste of leather and sour brass from
the tack room. Around Skye's face the pale fragrances of
her bedroom: Dove and Finesse and Teen Spirit. With
piss and the broken straw by her feet.

She was scouring the brush with the curry comb, in
short, angry strokes away from her body, standing below
the high, dusty window. When she dragged the brush
hard across the crib-rail, the horse edged away from her,
trampling the cement floor, yanking at its tether. She
turned through the hollow alarms of its hooves, speaking
softly, to soothe. She said, "Williwaw, Williwaw — easy
now, easy," and then "Williwaw" became a lament and she
went crying, her arms to the horse's neck, tugging the
great face down against hers. The gelding's ears went
back for a moment, and then his nose dug into her chest
and lifted up gently at her armpit. Her cheek leaned
against his, but her fist began to beat softly upon the blaze
between his eyes.

Her eyes were closed, the lashes dark and moist like a baby's. The smattering of freckles below them, the start of a dreaded blemish by her lip.

The tiny bones of her fist.

Williwaw let out a huge sigh through his nostrils. She dragged the sleeve of her jacket across her eyes and brought the horse-blanket from the crib, throwing it over him and unfolding it, front and back. When she crouched at the horse's chest to latch the front buckles, he bent and nuzzled her crown, the wide soft lips straying across her hair. She ducked round under his belly, tugging the back straps up through the wide rear legs, along the inside of his thighs.

Skye in her tailored riding jacket with the velvet lapel-flashes, her Christmas pride and joy. When no one was there but him she would still canter, instead of running, when they went down to the barn. Skye wanted to be a horse.

The barn was turning, receding around him. Unless *he* was turning, in the still, dizzy barn. It was a stage on an iron, spiral staircase, like the one in Auntie Cat's hall, and Skye was below him, in the tack room, sponging the harness. The saddle sat on its tree beside her, the gleaming stirrup drawn up to its flap. A hatch was rasping in the wind, somewhere up in the barn roof. She was holding the bridle, drawing the long reins carefully out through her fingers. Behind the partition Williwaw chewed at his feed. The voice that could not be Daddy's was counting, "TWO," from the haymow. "He mustn't die," she said, over and over, "He mustn't be dead."

There were dark sounds and light ones. The water lapped in his ears. His mother's bare arm cradled his shoulders. They had taken him out of his clothes and were bathing him. She carried the water up to his face in her left hand, spilling it carefully across his forehead and down his cheeks, caressing his eyebrows with her thumb. Her fingertips traced his nostrils, his lips, his eyelids, his ears; the polished nails that would tick on the piano keys whispered across his skin.

Her hand was at the waterline now, upon his chest, reaching towards his arm, and her hair fell down over him, spreading out on the water. "Jimmy," she said, "tie my hair back, please." His father was somewhere behind her, in the pink, steamy room; just a pair of hands with the signet cygnet signet ring on one finger, drawing the hair back, fumbling beside her neck. Her pupils were huge and shiny, they had swallowed the green of her eyes, and he watched himself, pale and floating within them.

Inside the water the flow of the bath tap trundled down. The water was hot but it could not reach in through his skin. His mother was squeezing and turning his hand, her fingers pressed and kneaded through his as if she were counting, or making him piece by piece out of clay. Her hand climbed his side and swept slowly across his ribs and along his belly. She held him between his legs, scooping and cleaning him, and then, as she lifted, the sudden release of her breath shuddered upon his chest. The tap water beat in his ears but there was the thin sound, too, of the open plug draining. The water escaped in a yellow spiral, he could feel it tugging at his heel, trying to drag a thin stream of himself down with it. And Mummy must understand, for her palm slid down over his shin to his ankle, and she lifted his feet from the danger, working her fingers into his toes, possessing him.

She was talking to him, or singing — he could hear her clearly on the other side of the water. She was taking him back to the time they had baths like this every night. But then she turned suddenly, and his face was lifted back into the air, and her voice was the ugly scratchy one that came out when she fought with Daddy — "For Christ's sake, Jimmy, would you close the door, there's a draught like a knife!" He heard the door shut. Was Daddy shut in or shut out? And she drew him against her again.

She pretended he was her baby. Hers and no one else's. His head was pressed up to her chin, and through his lips, against the soft skin of her neck, he could hear the sounds, *mmm-mm, mmm-mm,* that came up from her heart as she rocked back and forth. But he could not taste her skin any more; the smell of her powder, the lemon breath of her hairspray, had gone away. The bathroom had lost its smell; the memories lived in the smells. His neck and his knees and his elbows began to feel tight and lazy.

She must have known. For she let him go, all at once, and turned away, sitting alone on the floor with her back against the bath.

Perhaps she was crying, behind that metal wall. But he drifted and settled in the water, his ears back down in the world of dark, hollow noises. His elbows knocked against the sides of the bath; the engine-rumble of the tap died away. But the tight yellow whirlpool was tugging at him again, with that voice behind it crying "THREE, THREE, THREE."

Upside down, with the maple tree through an oval window tossing its branch tops at the sky. The old leaves coming off in twos and threes, sliding the way that you do in dreams, their rusty sails and fingers twirling towards him and out of sight. The little window was crusted and dull — if there was only some rain to wash it clean. And at once there were raindrops splashing and crawling through the dirt. And he thought *Wind in the Leaves,* and the leaves began streaming and tumbling from their branches. *Clouds for the Rain,* he thought, *Birds in the Sky.* An avalanche of cumulonimbus, cumulonimbus, cumulonimbus swept past the lower branches, piling up fast, with a long skein of geese fleeing before it across the window, their dog-cries tattered by the wind. He sent up a kite, though a voice inside him said "Don't be too greedy," and watched its blue wings tremble and slap at the air.

But he could not control the kite. It went out beyond him; it was trying to tug him with it, into the rain. It lifted and dived and sliced back at the wind, and its line snagged in the tree and came crumpling. It hung there, at the edge of his sight, pelted by leaves and rain, snapped up and dropped by the wind till its skin began tearing away.

The window shivered, and lurched off with him, dragging the storm clouds away from the branches. Everything rocked, and settled; he was a traveller. It was like going home at night in the car, waiting to fall asleep on the seat beside Skye, knowing that when you awoke the time and the distance would have passed; you would be home. And sleep would come, delicious, as the sounds around you, Mummy and Daddy in front, the radio music, Skye singing under her breath, drifted in and out, getting mothy and dim, your eyelids slipping down, moving through the night in a warm, safe room, the nicest thing in the world.

He could hear hooves beating on the road. Someone was galloping by beside them, shouting, something loud and fierce and indistinct. "A highwayman came riding, riding, riding . . ."; "All night long, when the stars are out, Why does he gallop and gallop about . . . ?"

But it was not dark, after all. Up through the little window there were other trees now, looking in on him and falling away, with more lining up to gaze down at him, dripping the slow grey rain down the window as they peered in, with the thick clouds behind them, though the wind had died out.

What were they thinking? What were they saying to each other? These were the trees along the driveway — there was the tamarack where the blue jays had nested, looming in with its wet, witchy fingers, brushing the glass as the car speeded up. They were talking about him and he wanted to stay and listen.

So he must somehow get to the window, and look back, before they reached the gate. The hoofbeats were so close, they were racing with the car; the man was shouting again; they were going too fast; gravel spat up against the floor.

He was pressed to the streaming glass. The house stared back from the end of the trees, with Mummy and Daddy and Skye standing in front, crying out to him, but the rain was in their voices.

The car dipped and swayed. The hooves beat alongside, the invisible horseman yelled from on high, like a command in a dream, but a command full of fear. "FOUR, FOUR," urging the wheels along.

They were at the gate. He reached back towards the house.

When things dreamed, nothing happened. Things were untroubled — a slow gathering in of memories that stood there, themselves. Nothing had to change. This was where he belonged, staring out patiently, as a tree — living or dying — could just stare out. As the walls of his room stared out at each other.

He would stay here forever. The wheels in the glass-fronted clock would run down and be still like everything else. The dust would settle.

It did not matter when the door swung inwards; he scarcely noticed. Their voices were vague, and muffled. Auntie Cat, with her arm around Mummy's waist, like people in a brown photograph from long ago. They came in, and left the door open, and the things just stared with him, contained and unaffected.

Auntie Cat was picking up clothes from the floor, and off the bed, folding them over her arm. She moved through the room and he wished she would not. He did not want her looking at everything. Things were not meant to be disturbed.

She was picking him out of his things.

Once he had sat in her house, in the carved chair under the spiral iron staircase, with a skein of aquamarine, aquamarine, aquamarine soft wool looped over his outstretched hands, while she sat before him, smiling, on the footstool, and wound the wool off into a big ball in her lap. Her round blue eyes that were always smiling but looked into your thoughts.

She ran her hand along the edge of the dresser, and his skin crawled. She fingered the wooden horse; he could feel himself being drawn out. She would wind him in and fold him over her arm.

He wanted to say, "Go away. You're a witch. You're not my Auntie." For she wasn't. Skye said Auntie Cat had had two husbands, and the last one had been Daddy. "You're not my Auntie," he said, his voice thin and spiteful in his own ears, but she paid no attention. Her hand closed upon the horse.

"I shall sleep here tonight," she said, with that wicked, strong kindness of hers. "That will be best for everyone."

He found his own horror in his mother's face, but she bent her head in submission and turned away. Why did she listen? He would not be left with Auntie Cat's eyes and greedy fingers. He had to go out with Mummy, trying to cry in her ear, to change her mind. But he was lost in the shadows as soon as she closed the door behind them.

The stairwell was a funnel of bars and reflections and false, unfamiliar angles. He was lost and thin and angry. He drifted too close to things to see them properly, and the only light was down over Daddy's shoulder, where his hand moved upon the paper.

The hand was angry, too. It sketched quick ruffles of brown chalk, and then cut into them with slashes of pen and ink. Daddy's breath came loud through his nose, and he pushed the paper around and away and pulled out another sheet. The black strokes were finding a hand, down at the right of the paper, and the chalk near the centre swirled around three crooked holes in an egg. The hand grew stronger; its palm faced out and the bony lines of its wrist slanted into the page. The paper lay upon the bed of the press, with the rollers and the thick worm gear black at the edge of the lamp's light. Daddy lit a cigarette and stared at the paper. When he blew the smoke out, the worm gear seemed to be turning. He pushed his chair back and went off into the shadows, to stand by the dark window.

The picture was going to be Skye's photograph. The one she took by the barn when he had his temper, when they told him to go in for bed and he didn't know she had the camera. "Oh you'll love this when you're thirteen," she mocked, when she got the prints. He was wailing, his hand was stuck out, his mouth pulled into a stupid, lop-sided hole. *"Poor* baby" — she had teased him for days until Mummy got firm with her, and then she had set it in a frame on her dresser so he'd see it each time he passed her open door.

But Daddy had just smiled, and winked at him; and a few weeks later had traded it from her for a drive to the trotting races; and the next day he had called him into his studio and they'd burned it in the woodstove.

And now he was bringing it back to life, out of the flames, out of his memory. In this room, drained of its smells, that was the only light in the house.

Daddy ripped the paper in two and crumpled it away. He bent over the copper plate on the bed. The metal curled away from the point of the burin, burin, burin, Daddy's Newfoundland pencil, under the clever hands that could turn things back to front. For the plate was a mirror, he said, and the mirror always shows you back to front. That's why photographs looked so strange.

The rollers waited, and the worm gear winked at the gleam of the burin and pretended to turn and start pressing him flat on the bed. "FIVE," it said, like a back to front echo of Daddy's voice.

Inside his room not one thing was quite where it should be. Auntie Cat sat on the bed, in her nightie, and everything had been moved just a little. The window was open and her clothes were folded on the chair. In a small half circle beside her were his seashells and his compass, and the parrot's feather from over his door, and the arrowhead from Oregon. On her lap were his pyjamas from under the pillow. There had been tears on her cheeks but her eyes were bright, and she was whisper-singing as she picked up each thing in turn. He could not feel her fingers any more, but she was stealing him all the same.

There was a soft, double knock at the door. "Yes?" she said, and put the pyjamas on the pillow. Daddy stood in the doorway, staring at her. "Cat," he said. "Oh, Jimmy," she murmured. He stood there. "You should be with Ailsa," she told him.

His hand played with the doorknob — "Ailsa's with Skye."

Auntie Cat turned back to the treasures on the bed-spread. "In that case, my darling, you should be with yourself." He watched her gather the trophies one by one into her left hand. Then he turned away, and the door shut quietly behind him.

Auntie Cat sat still for a very long time, before she began to put the things back, almost but not exactly where they had been.

There was no use fighting. As she moved across to the window, the room shrank in behind her. She leaned out on the sill, over the bare top twigs of the damson tree. "Shoo," she said, her kind face filling the window. "Shoo, now. Be off with you."

The voice said "SIX," and the night began tearing like a shirt on a rusty nail.

His ears were filled with the sounds of seashells. Their outside ticking, whispering slither. Their inside water and wind, and echoes that couldn't escape. There was so much light that everything was a mirror and hurt his eyes; the dunes and their manes of shining grass, and the sand by his face, and the white yellow sky.

The sky covered everything, but everything sounded closed in.

Beyond the dunes the waves were pouring, like one unbroken wave, and there was something drumming, inside the waves or in front of them. There was a rider on the beach, galloping off but getting no further away. The hooves echoed out through the ground; the sand grains danced on the dunes as if on a drumskin; the sky shivered under the hoofbeats.

The only thoughts here came in on their own, and left; you could not follow them, and you did not want to. There were people behind him somewhere, but it did not matter. It did not matter, it did not matter.

A little shadow began, at the edge of the sky, and there was a man coming over the dunes with a door in his hands, held slantwise like a kite. He walked slowly, in a wavering line as though looking for his way down the slope, and his feet crunched louder in the sand as he drew near. He settled the door in front of him, upright, so that it blocked out half the sky, and began to tap upon it. He was hidden behind it but his left hand was holding it steady at the top, while his other hand tapped with a hammer.

There was no handle on it, or latch, or keyhole. It was the plainest door there could be.

The hammer strokes stopped, and there was Chris Lamont's face looking around the side, with his thick eyebrows and his broken-rimmed green cap. He nodded, and gave a slow wink, and then picked up the door again and laid it down on the sand close by.

The nails stood up from the wood, bright and new. One by one the hammer came down on them and drove them in, top and bottom and sides. At each stroke the door stood up a little and the earth lifted up to meet it. Now the door stood open just a crack, and Chris Lamont was staring in, out of the light, with his hammer's head between his thumb and finger, and two square-headed nails held in his teeth.

The door closed to. The pour of the waves was shut out, and the seashells whispered and settled against each other.

The hammer beat at the door. *The clinch nail, the clench nail.*

The hooves raced by. The feathery clods of earth flew up against the door.

And "SEVEN, SEVEN, SEVEN," rang the iron gates of heaven.

♈ ♈ ♈

prelude

I was alone in the house when my sister called from England to tell me that our mother had died. It was not unexpected but, of course, it was unexpected.

I sat quietly on the couch, perhaps for twenty minutes, perhaps for an hour, and I saw — or imagined that I did — the progress of my mother's spirit.

That is what this story is.

The difference between the "gift" of a story and the gift of a poem (which true poets seem to experience once in a lifetime — "Kubla Khan" and "Everyone Sang" are the best known examples, probably) is that the poem comes as language: you are given the actual words; while a story unfolds like a movie or daydream in your mind's eye. It remains to be written. So I'm not claiming for a moment that "The Widow" was dictated by the angels. I had to work on it as I would on any piece of fiction — though for not nearly so long — and it is merely my *version* of what I experienced, as faithful to the original as I could manage.

It left me with the feeling — rightly or not — that I understood my mother better than I ever had in her lifetime.

The thought that our last desire and responsibility and act might be to search out the precise moment in our time on earth when we were most purely ourselves, is a peculiar and exhilarating one to me. (I wonder if I'll find the right time and energy to conduct that search *before* I die.)

And though the story ends with "extinction" it seems to me that as a fully-, indeed hyper-conscious choice it is by no means a suicide — it is an extinction *into* something, like those blesssd, conscience-free sleeps we commit ourselves to at the end of a long, achieved and exhausting day.

A dear friend on the West Coast, a nurse with more than twenty years experience, tells me about opening a window in the room whenever someone dies. She's a very down-to-earth person. She always feels the spirit departing.

THE WIDOW

The widow died, surrounded by gentle strangers. Their soothing voices, beneath the low-pitched ceiling, drowned out the birdsong from the garden and she found herself, out of nowhere, a cut-out, a black leaf flittering down a tunnel of light whose walls curved in and wavered around her.

It was silent, yet voices seemed to be chattering within her, agitating still more the shape which she had become.

A moth, a bat, a bird in a chimney. There were rents in the walls, but she saw only darkness. There were gaps too, from time to time, on either side, rounded like archways, but their lintels trembled and beyond there was only a black wind sucking.

And then, below her, was a different, grainier light, and she was hovering in a draught that swept down the tunnel, looking in through a smokey glass at her son's face. She could see him aslant, very close to her, huge, only the side of his face visible. He was older than she remembered, altered by private concerns. He was unaware of her, and she felt no need to reach in to him.

The wind snatched her off, and tumbled her past another dim window. A snapshot as though from a car passing at dusk. A mother and child, the child a woman already, facing each other across the room, absorbed in their worlds. The tilt of the mother's head was her daughter's.

She left them behind on the wind. She rose and fell and zigzagged in the lightshaft, till the walls billowed out to her right, and divided, and she was standing on grass.

She stepped forward, hesitant. Under the trees was a table set with a snow-white cloth; there were glasses, decanters and glass jugs, baskets of fruit. Young people stood talking, in open-necked shirts. The girls wore short dresses, their arms were graceful, their voices made of laughter. And he was among them, smiling, as young as *they* were. He looked up, still smiling as she faltered, the same smile, not a special one for her, though his eyes did recognise. They all turned round, to include her.

But she did not want that. She was awkward still, uncertain, a little dazed, and she wanted just *him*. He was hers, after all: his welcome should have been more personal. After the first relief at seeing him, and her quick wonder at his youth — he was just what he'd been when she had met him, a world ago — she wanted them to be together, separate: she was not ready for this company, this queer springtime out-of-doors. He should understand.

She stood her ground. Her eyes demanded that he come to her. She was hurt, angry, and he seemed not to notice. He would not notice. He smiled, and the other young people smiled, the group of summer girls, and their smiles reproved her, without meaning to, for her disappointment.

She was covered with shame. He was siding with them against her, he was *one* of them. Yet he smiled, happily, in his youth and ease, smiled even as she hung her head and moved away from the glade, hurt as an outcast child, wanting only invisibility. And like a child, to her further shame, she looked back for a moment and saw them still smiling, untouched by her pain, he too. She hurried away.

What were those girls to him? Did he think that he could have done better than choosing her? She picked her way, with her misery, through an open woodland; the light and the steady breeze between the grey trunks, the leaf-canopy overhead, translucent and veined from the sunlight, the cry of birds suddenly come into focus, made the misery hard to cling to. The ground sloped before her, her feet were whispering through last year's leaves, there were hints of blue pools (of water? of bluebells?) through the trees.

She had never been here, but was somehow familiar, as though it were blended from childhood scenes, or from picturecards come to life. She was aware at that moment of her young hands, of the effortless walking, of an almost forgotten tune humming itself in her throat. She could smell the place now, the fragrant, uncluttered breath of time past. Safe. She was wholly alone, she knew it, in this world.

And yet. Had she become a shrew after all, or a will unto herself, in their years together? An insistent, angry will that had tamed his heart? Somehow she could not remember enough. And was *he* so perfect?

She had lost him now, anyway. The cascade of shame and self-justification was stifled by this place. No one would judge her here, but herself.

She scarcely wanted to think of that life, which had been her whole life. How strange, but how simple. Like a dream that was not worth clinging to when you woke, or that you were too lazy and present-contented to retrieve. There were fields to her left through the trees, long open meadows that flanked the woodside and went down to the edge of a lake, or river.

Between her and the scene floated an image of sharing, of marriage, as a boat on the water, two passengers facing each other. Each had a pair of oars, each pulled in the opposite direction. There was a story-book drawing of Mr. Toad, upended in his skiff, oars awry as knitting needles, his legs kicking, and she laughed, like a wise child watching the grown-ups learning to learn.

Because, of course, both partners did not row at once, except in moments of conflict. You rested on your oars, while the other took over, and you imagined or pretended that you pulled towards the same goal. But no, when it was your turn you were going back again, in your own direction, looking at where you'd been taken, or at the other's face.

She was out of the wood, looking down at the lakeshore. Alone in the field was a hollow oak tree, seamed by lightning, the ground trampled hard and black all around it by sheltering cattle. She knew this place. Yes, surely somewhere around the lake was a ruin, the grey walls of an abbey or castle. She could visualise the old courtyard, with the sunken graves of the nuns, with pigeons strutting and the cry of jackdaws. She started to walk, diagonally down the field. There was no doubt that she had become a child, or almost one.

If the course was a straight line, or even if the river twisted and wound, there was still the question. If your partner had done the more rowing, and then that partner died or left you, or was stricken with illness, or you left him, where would you be in relation to the starting post?

It was like a puzzle that you had to get clear in your mind. A problem from when you first learned to do math in your head.

Did the survivor have to get back to scratch, to recover herself? Such hard work it would be to row yourself back, retracing everything. Back to front, too. She began to laugh at the absurdity, hopscotching down through the grass, because none of it mattered, here she was.

She found words to the tune she'd been humming. A thing she had learnt from the music sheets in her aunt's piano stool. She sang it when she walked out by herself when there were not chores to do, the younger children to tend, or schoolbooks to study. A silly song, a mighty foolish song, but it had gone with her into those precious solitudes. *Fare thee well, ye Mormon Braes, Where oft times I've been cheerie, Fare thee well, ye Mormon Braes, For it's there I lost my dearie. . .*

The singing brought back the dear scent of meadowsweet, and there at once were the cloud-yellow flower tufts, along the fence by the millstream. *So I'll put on the gown of green As a forsaken token And that will let the young men know That the bonds of love are broken.* "That's a frivolous song for Eileen to be learning," her mother had said, and her aunt had laughed. Her forgotten name came back, and was lost again, as she climbed the fence.

She looked down through her reflection in the stream. Water beetles sculled on the surface, little foam-packs clung to the rushes. Just once, at this time and place, she had believed in the wonderful safe absurdity of the world and her own aspirations. Though it was not safe, neither safe nor kind. Grief and separation, betrayal; the angels of pain, disease, madness brushing her children with their wings. But here, and then . . . *So I'll go back to Stricken Town*

*Where I was bred and born in And I'll find me a bonny new lad
To marry me in the morning . . .*

That was the time when you reached for experience,
through guesswork and fantasy. Not from experience, but
from stories, books, gossip, from intuitions and unsuit-
able songs. Were you ever so much yourself, before or
after?

She sat above the water, clasping her knees to her chest.
She rocked to and fro to her song, staring at the grey walls
past the mill. *There's as good fish intil the sea As ever yet were
taken* . . . And you knew then, as she knew now, that a
child, after all, could just cry herself to sleep.

The stream flowed below her, unchanged and
unchanging. Its syllables merged with the commonplace
words of her song. She was back to herself, completely.
She stopped rocking and leaned her face on her knees.
Felt the texture of the cotton dress on her cheek. Alone
with herself, one heartbeat before love.

She willed her own extinction.

ϒ ϒ ϒ

prelude

A week after John died, his voice was still there on his telephone answering machine: "I'm *not* available right now; but if you leave your name and number I'll get back to you as soon as possible. Thanks very much," — the rich, bitter baritone a ghost of the sardonic style that carried him through life.

He challenged the world to be honourable, generous and defined by ecstatic gestures; and so he condemned himself to disappointments upon which, in a strange way, he thrived, and from which he derived much of his dark energy.

I fear that his cancer fed on it, too.

He had suffered greatly, and gallantly, from his first treatment. His sense of life's ironies half persuaded him that he would get sick again. He had enough morphine tablets to choose his own exit, if the cancer returned.

I was not his closest, nor his most constant friend, but what we had shared over the years had earned us the right never to pretend. I would be with him if and when the time came to make that quietus.

In most ways I regret, even resent, that he submitted himself instead — without hope — to more radiation, surgery, and a hospital death.

A week before he died, his companion asked me to come and visit. I stayed in John's house, among his things, in company with his cat, spending four or five hours each day at the hospital.

John wanted me to read his diaries. Dozens of books were set out in his living room for me, almost thirty years' worth.

I didn't want to read them. I distrust diary-writing anyway, and in John's case all of that solipsistic grinding seemed a complete, stagnating waste of the energy which should have gone into the real writing he was trying to do.

The first evening there, shaken by my time in that fourth-floor hospital room, I took up a diary at random, flipped it open as I would a Gideon Bible in a motel room, and jabbed my finger at the page.

It was a passage about visiting his father, the near-mythic naval captain who'd abandoned his family when John was a child. The father was dying of cancer in Nova Scotia. He gave John his old sextant.

I didn't read any more. Each time I went back to the hospital I told John I was going through the diaries. He didn't believe me.

John's surgeon was an amateur sailor, with a boat in the Caribbean. John trusted and loved him. He confided in him. He believed him to be the best in the world. He took his advice on new treatments. He gave him his father's sextant.

The week John went back into hospital, his surgeon went sailing in the Caribbean. John grimly
professed to be delighted.

The work of technicians of the flesh is exhausting, and they need to take holidays and recreate
themselves. But when you allow yourself the mantle
of a technician of the spirit, you must take on the
whole responsibility.

John's cancer had spread to his brain, and cut off
most of the pain receptors. He was very much himself till almost the end.

It was a Salvation Army hospital. Every morning,
a brief service from the chapel downstairs was piped
through speakers into the patients' rooms. John
had a radio playing, softly and constantly, at his bedside. Two days before he died, a ragged version of
"Nearer My God to Thee" came out of the wall
exactly as Jimmy Buffett, on the radio, launched
into "Wasting Away in Margaritaville". I looked at
John: "Dare I laugh?" I said. "You'd better, mate,"
he whispered.

I told him I'd edit his stories and see that a book
got published. He didn't believe me. (It's *Harmless
Victories*, a Darkhorse Book from Exile Editions,
Toronto.)

I had to go back to Ontario. He was in the twi-
light already. Alone in that room with him, I found
myself talking about guardians, about a landscape,
and a road, about an animal companion. I don't
know where the landscape came from — maybe
from a dream of my own, or from a picture: there

was something of Redon or Bocklin about it, anyway. I began the story (which is his; I shall not go into it here) and remember insisting that the guardians *would* be there, when they were most needed.

I'd come to realize what a lonely soul John was — not just now, facing death, but as a chosen stance in life. His eyes were wary, his laughter pre-emptive, his gifts all challenges. But he was, as Yeats prayed to be at the end, "a foolish, passionate man."

The bedtime story I started for him seemed to touch on all that. It was, as well, a map, the start of a treasure hunt, a fairy tale.

And perhaps my story, "Guardians", is those things too.

I like the idea that the departing spirit is setting out. It's the dreamer, the clumsy youngest son, turned out of his house and home to wander off through the wildwood or ford the old river; to discover a world whose creatures and people are full of surprises, disguises, and innocent powers. A pre-neurotic, elemental world where, if your heart is true, you will come to a happy ending.

GUARDIANS

Down among the weeds, below the gravel shoulder, the earth was caked and fissured, a miniature livid-grey landscape of slump and erosion. His heels stirred up the surface dust as he jolted down; it rose and drifted back against him, coating his legs below the knees, settling on his shoes when he stopped, fine as talc. This dust, when the next rain fell, would become a potter's slip: a slick clay that would run from itself, exposing another face to be parched and blown and washed away in its turn.

Yet the weeds grew somehow. Their roots fumbled into this subsoil, and changed its nature. The lupins stood high as pines, in their own scale; the purple vetches had launched themselves over the tiny freshet ravines, and stitched an underbrush through them, snaring pockets of gravel washed down from the highway's shoulders, luring insects and seeds, hugging various tatters of human trash.

And in time, perhaps . . .

The diesel growl of the bus came back down the river, echoing off a rock-cut, the bus itself dwarfed and vanishing round the curve a mile away. The sound lingered, and surged, and was swallowed by the valley. The riffle of the shallow, swift water returned.

He sat among the weeds, above the naked stones of the embankment, and began to go through his pockets. He had planned to scrape a small grave for his things, but pushed them down instead, one by one, through the springy vetch canopy into one of the deeper ravines. He had almost nothing, but he meant to take nothing at all.

His driver's licence, the bus ticket, the pharmacy label; a faded restaurant stub from his breast pocket, perhaps from the last time he wore this jacket, with its smell now of closet and his own ghost-sweat, years ago. *Lepanto's 9/7/84.* Nine years. Two lives. His own archaeology. July 9th? September 7th? *Table 3. 2 Persons.* Who else? *$67.73.* No clues. Not even the name of the town. He made a tent of the papers and reached in his back pocket for his money.

He counted it, despite himself. A twenty, two fives and a two. He smiled at the thought of some drifter or hitch-hiker, later that summer, stumbling upon treasure. It was anonymous anyway, why should he burn it? He emptied the plastic vial, between his feet, and crammed the bills into it. The coins, too. A dollar eighty-two. He snapped back the cap and poked the vial out of sight through the vetches. The pills lay like a drift of candy eggs. He had three matches left in the box.

The sun was fierce on his neck, it glared back at him off the dry bankside, but he was cold through and through. As he knelt, he wrapped the jacket around him — so loose that he could pin it closed with his elbow while he struck the match. A brown worm crept up the side of his driver's licence; the flame in the sunlight was a mere shimmer of air. The printed words stood out for a moment, half of his name, iridescent on the crumpling black tent. A breath from the river scattered it through the lupin forest.

Orange, red, pink. The coating of the pills, as he retrieved them, smeared upon his fingertips.

So, then. He got to his feet, breathing hard, and made his way back up to the roadside. But his back was in spasm already, his lungs fluttered against him. Now that he was here, he began to doubt his strength.

Just take your time. He would treat the road as a border — across it was another land, with its own rules, and he would learn them. He fingered the pills, like beads in his side pocket. If he took one now, before he stepped out, it could only help.

He held it under his tongue, trying to make enough saliva to wash it down. It was bitter, beneath its pink shell, crumbling and soaking up the liquid of his mouth. A fragment lodged in his throat; he had to swallow repeatedly. He would need to find water, somewhere, up in the woods. His shadow reached almost to the white median line. And as though he had taken a pleasure-drug, the blacktop seemed brighter, more defined. It seemed to float, inches above the ground.

He stopped, in the sunlight, out on the highway, and lifted his face, breathing in. The bridges were burnt now; he was touched by a kind of unreal gaiety. He raised his left leg, in a prowling slow-motion step, flourished his hands and clapped them. He was an old negro man, doing the cakewalk on this long, shiny stage, laughing back at the world. His face rehearsed the vocabulary of childhood — all the stretching and twisting contortions of monster and clown. He danced to his shadow. His jacket swinging and flapping around him, he yipped and he cackled and he howled. His lungs had come back to life. Bent forward, on tiptoe, he ran and saluted the creature that shared his stage.

The porcupine lay on its side, plump as a stuffed toy animal, its legs pointing stiffly at the forest. Its eyes were half closed, a slip of grey tongue pushed out past its front teeth. He crouched beside it, and reached for its paw. It was more of a hand, or a flipper even, its smooth pads cold against his fingers, its sheaf of blunt claws not meant for flat earth, or for highways. A coarse odour, sweaty and close, came up at his face; he'd the quick sensation of being inside the creature's lair. Then he gripped the front leg, and stood, and set out for the trees, speeding up at the sound of a car rounding the bend. But the car had seen him: it beeped three times and pulled over. He hurried on. A voice cried, "One minute, please. Excuse me, sir. Yes!"

He stood, incredulous, trapped, the porcupine dangling from his hand. He looked up through the forest where he should be climbing. The car door slammed, and feet padded towards him. He waited; there was nothing he could do. And a face peered round, smiling up at him over the porcupine. "Hello, good day," said the face, Japanese and eager: "You have a beaver here, I think." Another door slammed, a cooing girl's voice came running.

"It's a porcupine," he said. "Ahh, *por*cupye," the face nodded happily, and turned to pass on the knowledge. "Ohhh" — the girl was broad-faced, smiling too, bobbing her head in greeting — "You shoot him?"

"No," he said, "no," not sure of their English. He made a vague semaphore at the road — "Car hit it. Killed it" — and held it up higher, by its hand, for them to see, finding himself making car-and-brake sound effects, nonplussed by this reality.

The absolute happiness of the couple beamed over him. "Please," the man said, taking his shoulder, "please." He turned as directed, towards the river, the man backing off across the blacktop, adjusting a yellow camera and waving directions to the girl. Who came laughing to stand beside him. "Okay," the man cried, "Okay, like that," and clicked the shutter. "One more," and he was smiling down at the girl, still holding the porcupine out in front of him. Click.

She tugged a red-and-black notebook from her shorts' pocket. "You write down name, please," she said. "We send you photo." And she handed him a pen, while the man scurried round, taking more pictures. Well, if these were the rules . . . The girl watched as he wrote. "Address, too, please, of course." Her feet were doing a little dance by themselves. This was insane. He wrote down Moira's address. On the facing page, in high-school script, the name of an RCMP corporal from the Huntsville detachment.

He succumbed to a little whirlwind of pleasantries. There was nodding and bowing, the notebook went back in her pocket, they laughed and shook hands, and the couple ran back to the car. Then she ran back again, and the notebook came out, and he wrote down PORCUPINE beside his own name. They waved and beeped, as they roared away, and he held up the trophy one more time for them. Then the road was empty, and he turned back to the forest.

It was the next stage, and perhaps he took it too quickly. The hill was not big. He could see the crest already up through the trees, but it was clumsy with moss-covered rockfalls, and he kept stumbling and slipping, losing his breath, uncoordinated. There was a thick feeling in his teeth, and his hand was in spasms from the weight it was clutching. He laid the porcupine at the base of a yellow birch, without due attention, almost throwing it down. Its meek, black face stared into the hillside. Exhaustion crowded out everything but the soundscape — the Jew's-harp whine of some chickadees below him, the rapid-fire knocking of a woodpecker. And by the time he took his second rest, sliding down with his back to a half-decayed stump, he could hear only the rasp of his breath, and the trundle of his heart at his eardrums. His arms and legs were shuddering with weakness.

He told himself that he had all day. A truck passed below on the highway, gearing down for the bend, and again for the climb up the valley, and he realized how much further he had to go, to get out of that world. But when he stood up, it was so much easier, like a second wind, and his feet found their way up and out of the trees.

He came out to bare rock — a flat, narrow hilltop dividing two valleys. He looked down over young trees to a crescent of water, the arm of a small lake. This was the Shield country he loved: moulded and stunted by winter, but glistening wherever he looked, in its summer skin. There was a place for him down there, waiting. Be calm, and he'd find it. Or it would find him.

He sat on the warm stone, his hands clasped round his knees: forgetting, and watching. The farther hillside, like a landscape jigsaw puzzle, was a shuffle of greens, with splashes of orange and red, premonitions of Fall, and the lances and penants of mature single trees jutting out of the skyline. Pale, spermy figures drifted across the sky wherever his eyes moved. A solitary bird cried out overhead; a raven drifting fast and high, dipping a wing towards him in recognition. *You'll sit on his white hause-bane And I'll pike out his bonny blue eyen* . . . He lifted his hand. "Look for me tomorrow," he murmured. And was smiling.

He thought of the place that was waiting, and himself dissolving there. If the mad, suicidal parasite that was eating its way through his ribs and spine were only *something,* itself. Something distinct that could tumble out of his bones when he was finished: like amber, enduring, or ambergris to breathe again on a rich woman's skin. But it was only him. *Or that the Everlasting had not fixed His cannon gainst self-slaughter.* He felt in his pocket for another pill, and squinted at it in the sun, between thumb and forefinger. In defiance of Hamlet's meaning, he had always held on to his first misreading of those lines — of God as a grim-faced gunner, slab-lipped, slouch-hatted, squinting down from a grey battlement into a forest clearing, menacing death with Death. *You take Mary, I'll take Sue There ain't no difference tween the two* . . . He chewed the pill quickly this time, getting it down before his mouth could dry up, squirming against the bitterness. A man was a sheaf of quotations, haphazardly ordered, to be read by no one.

The porcupine smell was on his tongue now, mingled with the opiate.

He went down towards the water, breasting through spruce and young pines no taller than himself; his feet stirred up a balsamy pitch-aroma, feeling their way around submerged stumps of the trees that were logged off here a generation back. The lake was no more than fifty yards wide, the water clear and warm where the rocks sloped into the shallows. Dragonflies crisscrossed, close to the surface; to his right was a thicket of willow-wands, growing from rock-clefts, rooted below the water. Some creature splashed and dived out of sight to his left — the ripples came round to meet him. He dried off his hands on his jacket. He would need water; he must look for something to carry it in.

The rocks were grey, a granite with dense white veins and sills, all smoothed to one surface by time and ice. But the outcrop beyond the willows was almost pink in the sunshine, with mica-flecks winking all over it. He skirted it, seeking the end of the lake, and saw, in the same instant, the yellow canoe and the three half-naked bodies that lounged by the water.

It was too close, and too sudden, to back away. The blonde girl lay on her stomach, facing him, her feet in the water. There was a glass by her outstretched hand. Her lazy eyes took him in. "Excuse me," he said, and gestured his surprise.

"It is okay," she said, "you can sit with us if you like. We shall not mind."

"No, no — I was just on my way round the lake. I didn't expect to see anyone."

The other girl was black — or her features, at least, were African: her skin had a reddish tinge, with yellow shadows, it seemed, stealing up from her ribs, beneath her breasts. She leaned on one elbow, against a small boulder, her long legs crossed at the ankles. She took off her sunglasses. "In any case, take a break," she said. "Sit down and describe your business." The blonde girl laughed and the boy beside her lifted a dripping wine bottle in salute.

"You see," he said, "we speak only English while we are in Canada. We conduct some bizarre idioms, maybe!"

The black girl patted the rock beside her: "Sit, sit," she ordered, and turned back to her friends: "So give him some wine."

The boy had a line of red beard along his jawline. Yet the hair which fanned out below his navel, from his skimpy white briefs, was a dense, flaxen scrawl. "We have no more glasses," he said.

The blonde girl slid her half-empty glass towards him: "He can use mine, all the same."

It was too strange to question. The rock was warm, the stillness, and company, seductive. He found himself savouring the sweetish white wine, while they idly talked and paid him no heed at all. "Are you students?" he asked, at last.

They started to laugh — everything seemed to set them off laughing together, as if the fact of their being here was some deep, shared joke. "Yes, yes," said the boy, "we are all students; but this month we are" — and he held up his forefinger, like a pedantic instructor — "fly-by-night tourists." He had moist, humorous lips, and his eyes were of different colours.

The blonde girl skimmed a cigarette package across the rock, without opening her eyes or lifting her head. "Have a Kraut cancer-stick," she growled, "and give one to Ulli."

He passed the cigarettes over and brought out the cigar from his inside pocket. "I was saving this for the end of my hike," he told them, "but I think I should smoke it now." His hand still smelled faintly of porcupine.

He struck a match, and reached over to light the black girl's cigarette. Her fingernails dug lightly into his wrist, and when she exhaled, the match went out. Even that set them laughing. He lit the cigar with his last match, and sat watching the blue smoke hover and stretch and then swoop away over the water.

"And where is this 'end of your hike'?" the boy demanded. His left hand rested on the blonde girl's calf. She shifted, and propped her chin on her hands.

"Up there, I think." He nodded towards the hillside behind them, across the lake.

"There will be a great view, alright," said the blonde, and laid her cheek back down on the rock. She yawned, her teeth white and even, her tongue strangely pink. "If you can find an out-look."

"In the meantime" — the black girl leaned towards him, with her pale palm outstretched — "you can, perhaps, tell me what is this." The body husk was intact, though the tail was crushed, and the miniature lobster-claws, bluish-grey with their smooth, tooth-like serrations, gaped on her slender fingers.

"It's a crawfish," he said, "or what's left of one." They stared at the creature together.

The blonde girl sat up abruptly, curling one leg beneath her. Her breasts were full and golden, the nipples dusky. "I will tell you what I think," she announced. "I think that every man, woman and child in your country must be given one square kilometre of this wilderness, to be responsible for."

"Why do you say that?" he asked, through the others' laughter.

She sniffed contemptuously. "Because," she said, and lay down again on her stomach, "and because I think so."

The cigar had gone out. He shook the empty matchbox. The boy stood, and came up from the water's edge, pulling a lighter from the waistband of his briefs and stooping to light the cigar. "Now," he said, "I will ask you a question," and turned back to face the lake. The shallow ply of his ribs showed through the skin. His arm sketched in the whole landscape: "Can you tell me what is the oldest thing in this place?"

"The oldest thing?"

The boy did not move. The black girl's eyes were teasing.

"Alright," he said. "Well, I guess these rocks would be the oldest things."

"No," said the boy, "you are wrong. Try again."

The blonde girl's laughter was deeper, less kindly than her friend's. Her green eyes were fixed on his, crinkling against the sun's glare. She reminded him of a tiger. "Try," she said.

He puffed twice at his cigar, and brushed it against the rock between his feet. The featherweight ash-nub began trickling, intact, towards the black girl's legs. She bent forward and blew at it gently; it swerved around her and rolled on down to the water. "Try again," she repeated.

It was easier not to resist. "Then the water, I guess."

She leaned back happily on her elbows. "Try again," she intoned.

"Very well," said the boy, "I will give you a clue." He was jiggling the lighter from hand to hand. "It is the oldest thing in this place, *and*" — and he lowered his voice theatrically — "it is the youngest thing too. Now you tell me."

"You call that a clue?" he laughed.

"An *excellent* clue." The black girl's voice was deep and affected, mimicking someone. Was it him? Or somebody they all knew, at home perhaps? Their laughter broke over him.

"Oh I don't know," he said. "The air? The wind . . . ? I give up."

Three grave expressions mocked him. Three heads shook slowly together.

"No. It is the *Echo* — watch . . . listen." The boy stretched out his arms towards the water and barked, "Hell-OH!" *Lo, lo,* came back at once from the opposite shore, and a moment later, *Lo-lo-lohh,* from somewhere up on the hillside. High behind him, out of the sun's glare, the raven cried down in response.

"Now it is your turn," the blonde said. "You must pay your penalty."

"No, no — wait a minute. How could there be an echo before the rocks?"

"It was waiting, of course," she drawled. "Is this not obvious?"

He was stung by her insolence. "It's not obvious to *me.*"

"Okay," said the black girl, "then answer me this: Which came first, the echo or the rock?"

"No, no," he said, "that doesn't work. The rock may create the echo, but how can the echo create the rock?"

Her chin lifted; she aimed a finger at his chest. "Suppose you were lost in the fog?" Her breasts were shivering with laughter.

"In the fog? You mean, if I were out in a boat, perhaps?"

"Very good," said the boy, "*Ex*cellent." He tossed the lighter, glittering, high in the air, and as soon as he caught it, lobbed it over to the black girl. She flipped it at once to the blonde, who snatched it one-handed out of the air and in the same movement, almost, sent it flying towards his face. He barely held onto it and then, with childish ferocity, he hurled it back. Their laughter went up, his mingled with theirs, and echoed across the lake. The third time around, the lighter went wild and he and the black girl scrambled to catch it. He got to it first. "End of game," the boy called. "It is yours to have for a keepsake."

"No, no," he said, and "Always you say 'No, no'," the blonde chided. "You must begin to say 'Yes, yes.'"

"No, *no*," he laughed, and held up the dead, half-smoked cigar. "I've had my smoke for the day. I won't be needing it." He made to throw the cigar off, into the willows.

"I will take it," she said, kneeling up. "I will smoke your cigar, and I will be Chancellor of our party." She came over on hands and knees, her full lips pouting to be fed the cigar, and her comical wink made innocence out of his eyes upon her body. Her skin gave off a light, peppery scent. She drew at the lighter flame and then sat back on her heels, face to the sky, loosing the smoke from her lips in a lazy purl.

He reached for the glass beside him, and toasted her clowning. The black girl began clapping, slowly and rhythmically, hands together, then hands upon knees. He realized that for the first time in six weeks he did not feel cold. He set the glass down, and clambered to his feet.

The boy was draining the wine bottle. He gestured with it: "One moment," and wiped his mouth. "There is one thing more that you can do for us." He rummaged among the clothes in the canoe's prow, and brought out a small camera. "If you please," he said, holding it out. "Come Ulli, come Katya." They slithered into a kneeling group, practised and automatic as musicians mugging for a film crew. The boy's arm lay upon the blonde girl's shoulder; his other hand brandished the bottle. The girls' hands rested together on the black girl's thigh. Their heads tilted, their eyes were huge. The blonde let out a perfect smoke ring as the shutter clicked.

He was half in love with them all. He wished he could carry that picture away with him, and the thought, somehow, was not bitter.

He set down the camera, by the glass and the lighter and the empty matchbox. "May I have the bottle?" he asked. "I want to take some water with me."

The boy's mismatched eyes were shrewd and gentle as the bottle changed hands. In the warm shallows the bubbles came gulping to the surface. The label began to lift from the glass. The water was clear, several feet out; a fish belly flashed for a moment, the stones of the lake bed swam into focus.

When he looked up, they were back as they had been when he arrived. The black girl had her sunglasses on, the other two lay together, face down. He walked past them, unacknowledged, and to the end of the rocks. "Well, goodbye," he said, "and thank you."

"You are welcome," the black girl spoke without looking up. "Safe journey," the blonde yawned, settling her cheek more comfortably on her arm. The boy raised a casual hand.

A moment later he had passed out of sight; the valley might have been empty.

And he was not cold. It was as though he'd become acclimatized. Above the treeline a cinder moon, a shade past the full, clung to the pale sky. He rounded the end of the lake, and began to climb. The wine lingered on his tongue. His breathing was warm, and regular; his back was supple; the odours of sap and bark, of dry moss and wild-currant flowers, breathed over him. When he stopped, it was to get his bearings, not from exhaustion. The slender lake was blue and unruffled below; there was no sign of the yellow canoe. The raven came back down the sky, planing under the moon's dead face. *O'er his white banes when they are bare The wind sall blaw for evermair* . . .

His grave was waiting for him, somewhere up there. Like the spot you drift towards in the woods, to make love in, it would find him.

He drank a little water from the bottle, and moved on.

If there was nothing, so be it. He would at least be one with the elements. And now that fate and outrage had dispelled themselves, and he had left all other calls behind — across the highway, at the end of a bus ride, in the brief, uncluttered letter on his desk . . . It was really too easy.

Once there had been forest, green upon grey, with the punctuations of ice and fire, and then forest again till the short, catastrophic ellipsis of the machines, and perhaps, again, forest. It was starting around him. And that echo? Waiting? He found himself laughing again, crying out like a child to the hillside. His *Ha* resounded, repeating itself, flocking out over the valley. There was no response this time, from the raven or down by the lake. The echoes retired themselves.

He veered to his left, towards the highest point of the ridge, following a dry stream bed like a path through the trees. It ended in a tumble of stones, dark-shagged with moss: a ruined culvert. Above it a flat shelf of ground, a clearing aslant in the hillside. He climbed up and found an old logging road, grassed over, with saplings of alder and willow in procession between the faded ruts. The air moved, up here, threading the young forest, smelling of pine resin. Almost at once he heard voices.

He came to the wilderness, and kept meeting people. The couple were just a few yards away, arm in arm on the trail. He felt dizzy; panic was close at hand. They wore shorts and hiking boots but drifted like Sunday strollers, so absorbed in each other that they nearly collided with him.

Their eyes focussed slowly, like dreamers wakened. He could find nothing to say. He stepped to one side, to make way, and the girl did the same. They dodged right and left together till she laughed, and put her hands on her hips. "It's like trying to get in an elevator," she said. "I'm not moving till you've passed!"

He chose to go round on the boy's side of the trail. He could sense the hostility; he had to say something. "Does this road lead anywhere?" As though mocking himself. No challenge, no edge. It would have to do.

The boy glared in distrust. His eyes lingered on the wine bottle, the city clothes. "Well the map says it used to go right round the hill." At a glance from the girl, his wariness faded: "We're supposed to wind up where we started, down at the old rail trestle." His hand reached out again for the girl's shoulder.

Her hair was trimmed close to her skull. Her skin looked as though it had never known makeup. "Which way are you going?"

He gestured: "I came from down there."

Her eyes were so clear, and healthy. "Are you lost?"

"No, no," he said, "I'm fine. I'll just take another path." For there was sex in the air between them; he had blundered in.

How young they were. But kind, as the young can be kind.

"Have you seen the red cliff?" she asked. "Have you seen the caves?"

"There are Indian pictures," the boy said, "right down by the waterline."

"I've just been wandering, so far," he told them. And smiled, stepping shyly back off the trail, to let them go.

"Just wait till you've seen the red cliff!" And she ducked in under her lover's arm as they moved off, throwing a bright glance back through the leaves to say their laughter wasn't aimed at him.

He went on, uphill from the trail. There were some old trees now, pines and maples, disfigured by wind or lightning, spared by the loggers, their bark smudged to eye-level by traces of fire. There was no true wilderness here; he would never find solitude. He couldn't go back, he could never recross that highway, yet the horror of being *found* was upon him now — the image of his dead face, a livid, dissolute bruise heaving up into the light at some hiker's eyes. And the carrying off of "the remains," the autopsies, enquiries, dental records, newspapers — worse, even, than what he had turned his back on, refusing the treatments.

And why this, now, this train of thoughts? It belonged in the other world.

The faces, too. And the names that came with them, and spelled their entitlement. Andrea, Moira, Robbie. He tried to banish them as they came — *I must be cruel only to be kind* — he had left them behind, he told them, at the end of a bus ride. Sparing them and himself. It was all in the letter on his desk. With perhaps a small postscript from Japan.

He was blundering towards the ridge. There were tears on his lips, shudders of cold in his chest. He could feel the cancer, a brain-like slug, a lamprey, flexing in his spine.

He was not strong enough, after all. Fate dogged him through the trees, rage clawed off all dignity. He collapsed against a low outcrop of stone. An old dog, rotting inside, panting his heart out. He could hear the sick air in his lungs, as if it surrounded him — a swampfull of creaking frog-calls and whistling birds. What would he do, stumble back to the trail? Cry out to the quavering echo? Or call for the two young lovers to come for him, and carry him down to Hell?

Beyond the stone was a shallow ravine, choked with creepers and dense young trees. He raised the bottle to his lips, his wrist ashiver, and felt the water spill through him as if he were glass, or metal.

The grave was watching, waiting for him to see.

An overhang of split rock, just below him, cloaked by the saplings. And when he slid down to it, a space beneath, like an animal's lair. Even the raven could not see into this place. It smelled of ferns, and darkness. The weight of his body helped him over the edge. The fall jarred his bones; a patter of earth followed after. The young pines sprang upright again, as he edged back under the rock.

The dark slash of stone; the sky beneath it, a thin, flat line; and the needle-fret of young branches, backlit and luminous from the day outside.

There was the sound of water running, somewhere, as if the little ravine were an ear for the hillside. And voices faintly, too; murmuring, laughing.

The reprieve from terror.

He wedged himself back against the rock wall, mocking the tumour. And spilled the pills out beside him, the fake-coloured candies, in a curving line.

He took them one at a time. A pill, a draught of water.

Was there a song line, *I'll die with a bottle in my hand*, or had he just made it up?

If there was nothing, so be it: he had always said that. But he'd lived with the vision since childhood — from a picture? a dream? — of the long valley that followed Death: a road curving at dusk along a riverside, towards a stone gorge, and the rush of a waterfall. And somewhere along that road, unvisualized but waiting nevertheless, the Guardians.

There would be riddles to answer, prescriptions to recite, before the gorge was reached. And an animal helper, perhaps, running on before.

He was warm again. The bottle rolled off, into the shadows. He lay in his green tent, hearing those young voices filter back from somewhere below. The rock was so gentle against his spine.

The green faded out. A girl's voice was crying out to Jesus.

He watched for the Guardians. They might bear cameras. They might be lazy, and naked.

ɤ ɤ ɤ

prelude

It would never have occurred to me as a child that my soul and my self were one and the same. My soul, I was given to believe, was my "chaste treasure", constantly threatened and besmirched by my sinful self. The image impressed on me by Sister DeSallis (rest *her* soul though she was a stern woman) was of something very like the Host — the communion wafer — a disk of white purity, blotched and invaded by my black thoughts and deeds. [Which is surprisingly like Loren Eiseley's microscope-view of this Earth, as the human slime mould colonises it.]

Confession and a contrite heart could shine it up again, of course. Briefly.

Yet was not the soul that ached through Purgatory, or writhed in Hell, or sang eternal hozannas to the Lamb, myself?

The questions began, naturally enough, around puberty. My self was becoming very important to me. My outrage and dread at the few deaths I'd encountered was at the extinction of a personality, of talents, of knowledge and memory (or are those the same thing?). That vacancy could be me! How could those things be mortal?

But if the soul and the self were the same, what exactly survived, if anything? (I hope I'm not sounding too solemn here — I'm trying to evoke

the earnest fourteen-year old that I was.) Would the
eternal Henrik Ibsen, for example, be the senile
dwarf that he died as?

It was too complicated for me then, and it seems
far more complicated now.

It's very tempting to believe, as people I've met
in Melanesia do, and as the ancient Egyptians did
that we have two or more souls apiece: one haunts,
one survives in an other country . . .

The old gentleman in this story has obviously
been thinking — in a more coherent way — about
those and other issues. People who live by the mind
have no concept of retirement; preserving consciousness and active thought to the end is vital to
him. He lives in a culture which, unlike ours, still
has some belief in the wisdoms that come with age,
experience and education; and wisdom is supposed
to be shared and passed on.

He's a self-appointed grandfather, for a day, to a
young man who lacks one.

What befell the dialogue twixt old and young in
our culture? Television, I suppose . . .

It's difficult to write a story these days in which
people *talk* a lot, and talk about what they think. It's
commonly regarded as "unrealistic" (and alas it is
now, in many circles). Yet the intellectual life is
important: Gully Jimson and Anna Wulf are as
"real" as Stanley Kowalski or Willy Loman; actually
they're more real — more brave, more generous,
more aware.

But to write such a story presents challenges that

are really quite comical. You keep feeling you should remind or reassure the reader that something is happening (*maybe I should bring in a waiter here; maybe someone should drop a glass, or blow their nose; maybe a dog should bark, a dove coo, a bus trundle up the street!*). I hope my solutions are graceful.

[Dr Redi's quotations are from Roland Barthes and Martin Heidegger.]

KEEPSAKES

The little town covers a Tuscan hillside, below a pass through the mountains, and looks out down a terraced valley where a road built by the Romans, or perhaps the Etruscans before them, crisscrosses the shallow river on twin- or single-arched bridges with low stone parapets.

When the rains come, the road turns chocolate brown; in high summer it is a tan-coloured thread stitching the river into place below the orchards and vineyards; but if the hard wind blows up from the south, along the face of the mountains, the dust from the road dulls everything under a grey coat — the young olive leaves, the roofs of cars, the washing strung between walls and balconies — and fills people's nostrils with a scorched, excremental memory.

Up this road a German division retreated, to make its stand at the top of the town around the higher of the two plazas, and higher still behind the old Benedictine walls where the small plateau of the monastery gardens allowed their guns to cover the road to Milan.

It was not the first time in their history that the steep and twisting streets had been the stage for skirmishes, duels and ambuscades while roofs collapsed into flame and the dogs ran howling, but the valley was shaken as never before by the new machinery of war which churned the river banks into soupy morasses and shattered the terrace walls, all the time hurling lead and copper and iron, ton after ton, into the hillsides and staring, abandoned houses.

The war marched north. The foreign armies departed. The voice of the waterfall below the first bridge could be heard again. The town recovered itself. The monastery was repaired and the townspeople's hands, with ancestral stoicism, built back the terraces and irrigation rills, doctored the trees and grafted new shoots in the savaged orchards.

But the earth was confused. A spadeful turned up in a garden or orchard might discover a Roman *denarius* lying closer to the surface than a Medici *scudo* or a British half-crown. Sometimes such relics worked or weathered their own way up into the light. It was a process the gentleman who sat each afternoon in the lower plaza, outside the Caffé Etrusco, understood very well.

Half a century after the battle, little drifts of shrapnel still moved through his flesh. A majolica bowl in his study back in Ravenna was half filled with the metal fragments his wife had picked out of his skin with tweezers, month after month through their thirty years together.

Now that he was grown so thin, the shoals of shell-dust were like cloudy tattoos on his thighs and buttocks and across his shoulder blades. Morning and evening, after the scalding baths which he took to bring warmth to his bones, the grey-blue particles lay like grit in the tub and had to be flushed away.

He'd returned to the valley five years ago and had spent each summer there since, renting the ground floor of a house in the lower town, spending most of his waking hours on the Etrusco's raised patio.

He was recognised now by the year-round patrons of the café. They greeted *il professore* with a cheerful respect, tinged with pity, and it was understood that the small table in the shade of the mulberry tree was reserved for his use. There was space there for his wheelchair to be tucked in and he could lean his right elbow on the table where his books were laid out beside the habitual glass of chianti.

He was so still, so seemingly absorbed in his books and in the notes he would make from time to time in a slender calfskin journal, that no one — except perhaps the *padrone* — realised how closely and intently he watched. If anyone caught his eyes upon them he offered a courteous smile, as if he were the one who had just looked up and found himself under scrutiny.

He was watching now as a young foreigner, eating alone on a bench by the café's door, went through a strange, internal convulsion. The boy's face reddened, he sat arrested, his mouth half-open upon a mess of pannini and cheese as a conflict of fear and shame broke out in his eyes.

He was an interesting case. He had turned up at about this time, the last two afternoons, to eat sandwiches with untidy haste, drinking beer straight out of the bottle, avoiding people's eyes. He was a cross and awkward youth, with no instinct for courtesy to the patio's waiter or the other customers, yet his unwavering sneer was so clearly the mask of a child besieged by self-consciousness. And he hid between the earphones of his portable music player, its clashing, monotonous rhythms sounding clear across the patio.

Now he lurched to his feet, fumbling money from his pocket to lay on the bench, and headed across the patio to the steps into the street. His beer sat unfinished, though he'd grabbed up the rest of his panini as he left.

He came into sight again, across the street, hurrying down towards the first bridge, beside the old mill race, his leather field-glass case banging against his hip, earphones askew upon his neck.

How old was the boy? fourteen? fifteen? The *padrone* reported that they were a family from Canada, staying for a week at a *pensione* up by the monastery. Just the parents and the boy, and the parents went off every day in a rented car. As for the boy — the *padrone* shrugged: "*Maleducato.*"

The older man was not so sure. The day before, the boy had removed his dark sunglasses for a moment, while he changed the tape in his little machine, and the eyes behind the surly mask were alert, and quite beautiful. The *padrone*'s own son, Tomasso, had just moved to America, and one might wonder how *he* had fared in his first few days if he'd stepped out alone from his uncle's house? Imagine this child as an immigrant, rather than a tourist, and — *dovrei avere compassione . . .*

But the boy was engaged already in a commando assault on the old mill, teetering along a rusted girder above the dry sluice-way, lobbing grenades into the sniper's nest that had pinned them down for three days. The panic which had launched him from the café was forgotten — the binoculars would of course still be there, he told himself,

lying where he had left them in the graveyard. No one else
was around, and he'd been gone less than an hour.

He dodged through the shell of the mill, between the
fallen beams, and the pigeons clattered up from their
nests in the walls as they had this morning. Then he was
out on the terrace which skirted the whole lower town,
alone in the sunlight where the crickets chanted and
everything seemed to drowse.

There were so many scents here — dry scents, for the
heat seemed to spring from the earth as much as the sun
— the soil was as red and baked as the roofs of the town,
yet so much was growing and every green smelled different. It was sexy. Well, everything was sexy.

He could not have explained to anyone — least of all
to himself — what he really thought about the world outside him. He held certain beliefs and notions, but they
were for the most part borrowed, and could change.

He lived through sensations, situations, the glamour of
things, in a vague but leapfrogging train of emotional
states, and would if he were honest have doubted the
truth of almost anything that he said. Yet he saw and felt
things more intensely than he ever had, or would again,
in his life.

Here, as the graveyard cypresses came into sight, was
where he'd stopped this morning to train his binoculars
on the third bridge. Imagining himself a German com-
mander looking down at the battle. And then that weird
bird had called, swooping close overhead, crying *pou pou*,
with its tiger-barred wings and crested wild face, and it
had led him, as he tried to follow it with the binoculars, to
the girl below who was also watching the bird, but whose
blouse was open to her lover, sprawled in the orchard
grass.

He could see where they had been lying. He could not resist it. He clambered down to the next terrace and went to the spot.

It was like an animal's lair — the twin body-forms quite clear where the grass was flattened, the pale stems at the centre like the parting in someone's hair, the dry earth showing through. He stared down. Just an hour ago. He was bewitched.

There were fruits on the trees around him: apricots, still green, though some had begun to ripen. The place smelled of them. He plucked one down, and held it to his face. It held living heat, the soft hairs on its skin teased his lips. One half of it was flushed, like Snow White's apple, the half that he tasted.

He knelt down where the man had lain, and put his palm, with as much wonder as lust, on the place where they had joined. Their heat in the heat of the earth.

Something grey, not a stone, lay just by his little finger. The zigzag lines on it made it stand out. A shard of pottery, not much bigger than his thumbnail, from the rim of a cup or bowl. Its rough skin drank in a smudge of apricot juice from his fingers. This would be his souvenir. He got to his feet and dropped the little fetish into the binocular case.

The wall of the graveyard stood above him: between those two cypress trees he had lain and spied. And here, ten feet below the buried dead and the dark trees which fed upon the graves, he had watched "the act of generation".

He laughed, and set off to retrieve the spyglasses.

They were gone. There was his form in the grass, and the dry yellow flowers that smelled of curry; and there was the white slab he had lain beside, and read when the lovers had gone — the grave of a young girl, with a poem nineteen lines long carved upon it, each line ending with *Clara*. But the binoculars were not there. Anywhere.

Tears sprang into his eyes. He sat on the grave, quite honestly unsure why it mattered so much. The fact that someone had watched him, and could be snickering at him in the town? The explanation he'd have to make up for his father? Just having something stolen? No. He broke off a few of the curry flowers, and put them in the binocular case. He didn't know why. And the tears wouldn't stop till he got up and left the graveyard — he'd shamed and betrayed his grandparents, and this was his punishment.

He walked slowly back into town, and up towards the *pensione*. If his father asked he could say the binoculars had been stolen — well, they *had*. He could half tell the truth and say that he'd left them somewhere, birdwatching, and couldn't find them. He didn't want to deal with his father, didn't want to see those eyes disappointed by a lie they could not understand. Most of all, he didn't want to feel this guilt.

He had just passed the café steps when he felt a hand on his arm. It was the waiter from the patio, gesturing, "*Venga, vieni.*" He followed him up the steps: perhaps they would give him a beer, for the one he had left unfinished. Up on the patio the café's owner stood waiting: "Come," he said ungraciously, "*Il professore* he like to speak with you." He led him towards the table in the tree's shade.

The old cripple with the white face was smiling up at him, extending a hand. "Filippo Redi, *dottore*," he said, his voice incongruously deep, and soft: "You will excuse me if I remain seated." The hand was like a thin glove over bones; you would not dare squeeze it.

"What do you want?" the boy asked and then —
because he really did not wish to seem rude, especially
since the *padrone* showed such deference to this old man
and was glaring now at the boy's demeanor — "*Scusi*," he
said, and mumbled his name, "but how can I help you?"

The old man folded his hands on the light rug cover-
ing his legs. "Please, please be seated," he said. "I would
like to buy you something to drink, a small 'bite to eat'
perhaps, and to take a few minutes of your time in conversation."

His speech was gently accented and deliberate. Was
that his illness, or his carefulness with the language? The
boy sat down. "Your English is very good," he said.

"How kind of you. You are much *too* kind. I regret that
English is not my most fluid tongue." His face had been
full once, perhaps — there was loose skin below his eyes
and at his jawline. The dappling shade of the leaves
played on the bare scalp.

"So how many languages do you speak?"

"Ah. I can only, with honesty, lay claim to five."

"That's amazing," the boy said. "Why don't you get
them mixed up?"

The man leaned forward intently. He had green eyes,
and it was hard to imagine what he'd been like when he
was young. "It is said," and he paused for a moment,
checking the boy's face. "It is said that the truly original
mind, the *inventive* mind, never ceases to explore the
world through the mother tongue. For those like myself
who are — let us say — clever, I think is your word, *clever*
but not truly original, (some would use the old Italian
word *dilettante*, which in fact means to delight in something, which is not so bad, heh?) for us, the exploration
of other languages — their genii, their different ways of,

of appre*hending* the world — is our best path to understanding."

The *padrone* hovered without impatience; he listened in awe to the sentences unfolding in another language. The boy was more eyes than ears; the repulsion he'd felt at the old man's closeness was shifting to fascination.

"Well, well — now you understand why they call me *professore*, though I have not stood in a lecture room for twenty years. Perhaps I have written things which might be instructive. I hope so. And now we must provide you sustenance."

The *padrone* moved closer. But, "No, excuse me," the old man intervened, "forgive me, but you should not drink beer, as I have observed you to do, not in the afternoon — it will muddle your wits.' There is a saying in Tuscany," and he rattled off something which set the *padrone* laughing. "In essence it says that a man who drinks beer in the afternoon is good only for siestas or — for something else.

"Do not be offended, please, by our laughter. Signor Portali will bring you food and drink that you never would find in Canada. 'When in Rome,' *si?*"

The old man seemed quite at ease in the silence that followed. He reached for his notebook and on a page that was crowded already with tiny writing he began a new entry. But he did look up once, and smiled into the boy's eyes as if they shared in a happy secret; and strangely enough, when the boy looked around the patio, he got nods and smiles from a couple of tables.

The patio waiter approached with a tray, and the notebook was put away by the pile of books on the table. "It would please the *padrone*," the old man said, "if you followed our custom of removing our hats when we eat."

The boy grinned, and took off his cap. "You sound just like my mother."

"Ah," said the other, "an old woman, *si?*" And then ducking his head, holding one hand up in protest: "No, no — no offence. Believe me, I understand. I do take a delight in the small vernaculars and I know that in English 'old woman' means *fussbudget* (am I correct?) but it also means 'wife' or 'mother', yes? 'Old lady', too. Such a language!"

Now his eyes flicked to the earphones, and when they too had come off, he sat smiling while the waiter set down tall glasses of *orzata* for them both, a demitasse of espresso by the old man's elbow, and in front of the boy a tray full of tiny appetizers.

"Wow, thanks," the boy said, "this looks great." And then, "What are you smiling at now?"

"I am actually watching the bones in your face, the bones in your wrists." And the smile grew wider. "I am thinking of that peculiar word 'rawboned.' *Rawboned* — are you familiar with the expression? I have noticed that in English fictions the Canadian male is most often described as 'rawboned'. I am pursuing its meaning!"

Ironically, though, that smile exposed the man's teeth, up to his gums, as though the skull were leering through, eager to take over.

"And now, if I could persuade you to remove, to *doff,* your *mafioso* sunglasses, we could perhaps have a conversation."

"Okay," the boy said, and began on a saucer-sized plate of crushed olives and some kind of fish. "What shall we talk about?" The salt and the spices brought saliva springing from every part of his mouth. He reached for the glass of soda: it tasted of mandarins, though it was clear. He drank half of it down.

"Taste, *taste* — give your palate a chance, I beg you, to savour our food."

Yes, an old woman, but generous too, and —

"Tell me, did you recover what you had lost?"

It was strange, like watching a Japanese film and forgetting, after a while, that the faces were foreign. The wasted body, the skeletal hands, the total pallor of the features had yielded already to the personality of this man, this talker, those searching green eyes. And now — did he have the binoculars?

"Why do you ask me that?"

The man shrugged: "I saw, when you were here before — I saw the distress in your face, and I thought, 'that young man has left something behind, and now he will have to rush off and retrieve it.' And you did rush off, and you interrupted a meal, which is always a bad thing to do, and my hope is that you will find this small repast some recompense.

"Now, if I may suggest: try that morsel of *buffalo mozza* — there, mounted on the slice of tomato. It is exquisite, believe me — quite the best."

But the question was not forgotten, nor was the boy's impulse to confide.

"I left some binoculars in the graveyard. They're gone."

"Ohh. That *is* a misfortune."

"No, they were my grandfather's, you see. It's not like I can replace them."

"And your grandfather will be distressed — angry with you perhaps?"

"No, he's dead; he was killed in the war. It's — I don't know really . . . " He wished he had kept his mouth shut.

There was a clamour of voices from across the patio: shouts, whistles, cheers. The waiter came scampering by like a child, doubled over with laughter, and a volley of bread rolls chased him through the café doorway. A huge man was dancing, beer glass in hand, round and round upon one leg, while his friends beat time on their table, until he finally fell, but held his glass triumphantly aloft. He toasted them from where he lay: "*Salute, professore!*" The old man raised his glass. "*Salute, Americano!*" The boy raised his: "*Canadiano,*" he called. "Ah, *Canadese,*" the man boomed, "Pea soup, CPR, Gordie Howe!" He lumbered up and approached them, but some small gesture from the old man changed his mind. He gave a flamboyant salute, winked at the boy and went back to his friends.

The old man touched the little coffee cup to his lips. "These are soldiers," he murmured. "They are just home from Jugosalvia; they have perhaps met some of your compatriots there."

"Good only for siestas or — something else?"

"Bravo," the old man nodded and nodded. "You are 'acute', I believe is *le mot juste*, or is it 'astute'? No, 'acute' it must be. I shall have to teach you the original proverb before we part. And by the by, the American word 'cute', did you know?, it derives from 'acute', and my good friend Professor Powers of Trinity College Dublin assures me that in his country 'cute' is still employed to mean 'sharp' — in reference to a man's mind, or to a knife."

He moistened his lips and placed one hand flat on the table. "Attend," he whispered. "About your grandfather's field glasses." The boy leaned forward.

"My young friend, these things that we treasure, these objects charged with memory and significance, you must learn that they — how shall I say? — they *walk away* in their own time. It is true. I suspect that they move into limbo, but if not — if they fall into the wrong hands — do not fear for their purity. They cannot be defiled. Their *vertu* departs from them and they are merely objects again."

He winced, as if a cramp had taken hold of him, and leaned back from the table. "And sometimes," he continued, "we find that the time has come to give such things, such treasures, away. They are no longer ours; they have work to do elsewhere. If you do not understand what I am telling you, at least try not to forget. One day you *shall* understand."

"This is different," the boy said, "none of us knew him. He died before my father was born. My brother's got his medals — my dad gave them to him when he left home. I got the binoculars from my grandmother: she only gave them to me last week, before we left. That's all there was, except photos."

"Ah, photographs." The old man reached for his notebook and drew it towards him. "Tell me about your grandfather's photographs."

"Well, there's the one on my grandmother's piano . . . "

"*Si?*"

"Well, just a young guy in uniform, looking off into the distance. He had a moustache."

"In uniform? I find that strange, my friend, strange but — *typical.* That public disguise, that *sacrifice.* Surely your grandmother knew the man behind the uniform. Surely she had memories more human than that . . . "

The boy had the sudden vision of his grandmother young and naked, in the arms of her husband — of her fiance. It seemed quite natural, a different thing altogether to imagining his parents. He knew they were making love often on this trip — maybe out in the fields like the couple this morning, but it made him cringe. His grandmother, though . . . he thought of the picture of *her* on the piano, nineteen years old. Patricia."

"There is a Frenchman," said the old man, "a *thinker*, I would call him; he is too playful to be called a philosopher. He has interesting things to say about photography. He claims that because of the photograph our species has lost the ability to conceive of the *sequence of time*."

"I don't understand."

"That is all right. Just try, if you please, not to forget. Certainly you will understand one other thing he has written. He says — I will do my best to render this in English — he says, *A photograph of the deceased touches me like the deferred rays of a star.* That is very fine, do you not agree? Now I will show you a photograph."

What a character, the boy thought. What a weird mind. As the old man carefully opened his notebook and drew a small envelope from a flap in the cover, the boy was trying to imagine meeting someone remotely like this at home, trying to imagine how he might meet him if he did exist, trying to imagine sitting like this, in a Burger King, and listening.

"Now that is my mother, Francesca Redi, *née* Porelli. The year is nineteen hundred and twenty, the year of her wedding. The place is Ravenna."

The little photograph, trembling slightly in the hand which supported itself on the table, showed a young woman in a short dress on a balcony, turning to smile at the camera, her hair styled to curve in and frame her cheeks."

"She's pretty."

"*Is*, yes, that is the word precisely. For us she is dead many years, in our Italy of television and jet aeroplanes, fifty years after a war she could not have imagined. Yet there she is, as you say, and pretty, as you say, and the Kingdom of Italy — which is lost beyond dreams — stretches before her beyond that balcony in the eternal sunlight."

"That's very poetic."

"Ah, no. I translate poetry. I understand it too well to imagine that I could compose it."

The old man replaced the photograph in its envelope. He leaned back in silence while the waiter, who had appeared with fresh glasses of soda, removed the tray and wiped the table, skirting the twin pile of books. "*Grazie*," the boy tried, "*Bene.*" The waiter smiled, and murmured "*Ciao*," as he departed. "I thought *ciao* meant goodbye," the boy said. "Ah yes — goodbye, hello — literally it means *your servant!*"

A narrow shudder went through the old man's body. The little envelope began shaking in his fingers.

"Let me help you," the boy said. He stood up and leaned over to take the envelope and the notebook. A faint, fungusy odour came from the man's skin. "*Grazie.*" "*Ciao.*"

The boy took a drink of his soda. Was the old guy having some kind of attack? And who looked after him, anyway? But the moment seemed to have passed: the bony hands lay folded again on the rug.

"Have you always carried that photo of your mom?"

"Ah, no. I 'dug it out' as you say, before I came up from Ravenna last month. A man who is close to death always thinks of his mother."

"Are you — 'close to death'?"

The old man smiled. "I do not wish to depress you. Young people can be so sensitive. The point I was making is this: I shall be buried beside my wife in Ravenna, as we both desired; but I shall sleep in my mother's arms."

"Do you believe that?"

"Hah!" The old man leaned his head on the back of his wheelchair and spoke to the branches above him. "I have yet to arrive at any firm belief. Nor do I wish to. It seems to me that we must believe many, contradictory things, or we cease to be human."

He looked down again. "Please, enough about me. Tell me something of yourself — or, if you prefer, tell me about your parents. I see them every morning, but then they are gone — without you. They have brought you with them, but they do not know what to do with you?"

"I guess so — but it's not their fault."

"I implied no fault, my young friend. To find fault is to value the frame above the painting."

"Yeah, well, they were due for a holiday, and my dad always meant to come and see his father's grave."

"His grave?"

"Yes, this is where he was killed. So we saw the grave in the war cemetery, and the place where he died, and now they're exploring the district. Two more days."

Somehow, without his noticing, most of the customers had left the patio. Outside this half-circle of shade the afternoon sun blazed full on the tables. He had reminded himself of their first day in the town, the walk by the river through the cemetery, with its trim lawns and uniform white stones and his own name, when they found it — *he* found it — somehow unreal. The flowers they had laid were the only ones there, except for the beds of geraniums round the cenotaph. But then came the drive to the third bridge, where the trout swayed among the weeds in the parapet's shadow and where his grandfather's blood must have flowed. And his father then, lurching towards him like a frightened child, all arms and eyes, offering him weakness, which he could not repond to but his mother could, drawing her husband's face, with its tears, down against hers, while he turned back to the fish, and the swallows skimming beneath the arches, and wished to be anywhere but in their company.

He looked up. The green eyes were watching.

"I should perhaps tell you that I too was a part of that — engagement. Among the defenders of the town."

"But you're not a German."

"No, no — how to explain the confusion. You see we had two governments then in Italy. The new one in Rome was at war all at once with Germany. The old one, up in Milan now, stood as before, on the German side, to fight off the invaders.

"You cannot expect too much of young soldiers — 'soldier boys' as I heard an Englishwoman once call them — except for loyalty to their comrades."

But the boy was barely listening. "Were you in the fighting by the third bridge?"

"Yes, there, and then at the mill, and then in this plaza, retreating all the time evidently, and at last, with nowhere to go, at the monastery. Very few of us were there to fight at the monastery when the tanks came to 'finish us off'."

"But you were at the bridge."

"As I said." Then he drew breath, and let out a long, low sigh. "How foolish of me. It was there your grandfather died, *si?* I am sorry. But as for what you are thinking, it is not so likely. And really, if it were the sad case that I

— well, very soon we shall be able to laugh about that together, he and I."

"Do you think he'd be laughing? How — I mean, how must it feel to see your child growing up without you, to see your wife — "

"No, *please!*" There was a fierceness in the old man's voice that cut him short. "No, no, no — even for an Italian Catholic that is too absurd."

He swallowed twice, with real difficulty it seemed, and beckoned for the boy to lean closer. He spoke very quietly: "How could they *bear* to be watching? Can you *imagine* the state of impotence? You have just described *Purgatory*, young man, a Purgatory beyond Dante's imagining."

"Yeah," the boy grinned, a little scared by the intensity in those sick features. "I guess that is kind of stupid."

"You think that your grandfather watches you in the bathroom?"

"Hah! I sure hope not!"

The green eyes flickered with laughter, tracing his thoughts.

"Attend. The love, the concern, the protection is the part that we leave behind when we die — as a benediction, a blessing, *si?* It is alive, I believe, in this world." He cleared his throat, the adam's apple trembling through the loose skin. When he spoke again, his voice was harsher, thick-tongued. "Of course they — the dead, we — leave other parts of ourselves, too. Parts that have loved this world, perhaps, all too much."

The old man was obviously feeling discomfort. He reached for his glass and worked his tongue through the bare mouthful he took. "I should not have had that espresso." He ducked his head and shrugged, in mock guilt: "The pleasure principle, it will just not lie down and die." And then, looking off towards the valley, "Has it ever occurred to you that the soul is a stranger to the self?"

His voice was different, his eyes had strayed off, there was no point in trying to respond. But his hands were plucking at the rug in agitation, and one of his legs, you could see, was shivering.

"I shall have to ask a great favour of you," he said, bringing his eyes back with an effort to the boy's face. "I am most sorry. I must ask you to help me — to help me to reach the lavatory. Forgive the discourtesy." His brow was drenched in sweat, his whole face was damp.

Oh god, the boy thought, he couldn't imagine anything more scary or disgusting. But he was trapped, wasn't he? *Do I have to undress him, will I have to wipe his ass?*

He got up and edged himself round the table, past the tree's trunk. The old man was breathing fast, but contrived a smile. "It was the Englishman Coleridge," he gasped, "who imagined with horror a human mind trapped in the body of a fly." Yeah, I saw the movie, the boy thought, and then, as he shifted the wheelchair around, "Ah," cried the old man, "saved by the bell!" The white face lolled back to stare up at him: "*b - e - l - l - e!*"

And there stood the girl from the orchard.

The blood rushed so fast through the boy's face that his scalp grew wet. He had seen her breasts, he had seen the inside of her thigh, seen her thrusting back at her lover, her fingers clutching those buttocks. But now she was only concerned, running forward to kiss the old man on his brow, those same fingers stroking the palsied wrist, soothing.

She looked once into the boy's eyes, and dismissed what she saw. She pulled the wheelchair out towards her, and swung it quickly around. "Do not worry," she said as she steered the chair towards the café door, "he will be fine, fine."

An old hand lifted, a feeble papal salute, as she manoeuvred the chair inside. She was all brown skin, the short cotton skirt celebrating her legs, the sleeveless blouse her arms, and he was free to stare until the door swung shut.

The patio was empty. He retrieved his earphones and cap, and when he stepped out from the shade a dizzying 'head rush' came over him. He reached to steady himself on a chair back — it was too hot to be touched. He walked slowly across to the steps, and down into the street. The light off the house walls was blinding.

What time was it? He had no idea how long he had spent back there.

"Hey there! Hello, you! Come back!"

The girl was standing, at the top of the café steps, beckoning to him. She came down two steps as he returned. She smiled down; he could see almost to the top of her legs.

"My uncle said that you would leave," she said. "He demanded that I intercept you."

Where the old man's vowels had seemed English, hers sounded American.

"You speak English too?"

She put her hand on the railing. "In my family there could be no choice. Besides, only Yankees and Anglos could be so lazy as to trust one language."

"Shouldn't you be with him?"

She tossed her head. Her hair flew back like a shampoo commercial. "He needed his medicine. He's okay. I will take him straight home."

The boy stepped closer. Partly he wanted to take his eyes off her legs. Now they had to avoid her breasts. And her eyes laughed at him; whatever she consciously thought, they were saying *You're a kid, I'm a woman, understand that and we'll be friends.* Yet she couldn't be more than eighteen, maybe.

"He's your uncle, then."

"Great uncle. Same difference. But listen, he invites you to dine, a genuine meal, before you leave."

"Tonight?"

"Ah, no." Her eyes became darker, confiding. "The medicine he must take, he says it makes clouds in his head, you understand?"

"So when?"

"Eleven, eleven thirty, is okay? In the morning?"

"It's our last day tomorrow," he said. Her eyes were really amazing. "I promised my parents to go out with them."

"Too bad," she shrugged. "My uncle thought we would have a good time."

"I'll ask them then — they won't mind."

She came down, to the step that he stood on, and folded her arms, leaning back against the wall.

"Understand this," she said. "Me, I am 'two-a-penny'; my uncle is a great man."

"I've never met anyone like him."

Her laugh had a disconcerting rasp of vulgarity. "He thinks you were sent."

If his parents were put out or hurt they didn't show it. "At least," his mother said, "we'll have the three days together in Florence. And you'll really love it there." And his father asked, "Is this friend of yours — forgive the expression — *respectable?*"

"He's a cripple, Dad," the boy said, "and he's some kind of university prof. He speaks a zillion languages; he talks like a book. I like him." He felt uninclined to mention the third bridge — or the girl.

They ate that night at the *pensione* and then went out with the other guests onto the narrow balcony to watch the moon come up through the pass. The town's shadow filled the whole valley with darkness till, little by little, as the moon crept over the monastery walls, the shadow was drawn in towards them and the tiled roofs below swam in moonlight

"It's so goddamn peaceful," his father said. His mother's hand covered her husband's on the stone balustrade.

When they had gone to bed he spent half an hour in the darkness of his room, leaning on the window sill. Here and there down the valley a metallic gleam picked out a bend in the river; otherwise the moonlight was like mist on the terraces. There were few lights anywhere and virtually no sounds, except for the waterfall's hush. A bonfire was burning, though, off to his right — a glowing smudge in what must be one of the orchards . . .

He thought of the nest in the grass under the apricot trees.

There was a double tap at the door and his mother was there, tentative in the doorway, hands in the pockets of her dressing gown, feet bare.

"It's not much of a holiday for you, is it?" she said.

"I'm fine," he said, and, "You're the one who needs a holiday."

He turned from the window. The light from the corridor slanted across her face. He was quite conscious of things changing. He felt the old tug of her concern, drawing him towards her breast, but he could see himself, as if through her eyes, solitary and unreachable by the window.

"I should be worried about you," she said.

He laughed — a kind of laugh. "Forget it, Mom." The gold chain with its locket glinted at her breastbone; he realised that she was naked under her robe. "Go back to bed," he told her, speaking as he might to a child.

She lifted her chin: "We're on your side, you know."

He turned back to the window. "Of course you are," he said.

The door closed softly. He shut his eyes for a moment before he looked out again at the night. A bat swooped up past the window and tumbled away towards the rooftops. He saw another, then another, and from somewhere below the plaintive madness of a cat's cry, like a soldier lost in the mud calling *Help*, sounded and kept on sounding.

He watched, as he undressed, a cloud swallowing the moon the way a snake swallows a frog. "Taste, *taste*," he declaimed. "Give your palate a chance, I beg you, to savour our food." He made it onto his bed with one leap, flinging himself back upon the pillow. "It is exquisite, believe me," he told the ceiling, " — quite the best."

He started to think about the girl's thighs, but her face got in the way.

They were walking down for breakfast at the car park's café when he saw the wheelchair approaching. The girl's face was close to her uncle's as she leaned forward, easing the wheels over the cobblestones. She was talking, and laughing.

"That's my friend, Dad," he said. He could not avoid introductions. The old man seemed tiny out on the street, slumped down in the wheelchair with a light rug, in the same pattern as the one that covered his legs, draped on his shoulders.

The boy saw with surprise that his father instantly took to the old guy. In fact he saw more to like in his father than he had for a year or more. There was a lack of phoneyness, an easiness with who he was, a grace in his body. If it had been someone else's father he could have felt envy. But his mother was repulsed, even scared, by the meeting. He felt her distress when she took the old hand. Yet it was she who made conversation and lingered, full of polite concern and gratitude.

"It is I who am indebted, Signora. Imagine the generosity of a young man to indulge an old scarecrow."

The girl stood, smiling and distant, in a blue sundress and wedge-heeled sandals, waiting for them to move on.

The sun was already too hot; there was no movement in the air; the sky seemed more white than blue. They ate beneath the café's awning, and the boy introduced them to *orzata* sodas, discovering that there were fifteen different flavours.

"Your friend is very refined," said his mother, "but oh, Stevie, he's at death's door."

"I think the Professor's companion's the main attraction," his father said. And relished his son's blushes.

"Don't tease him, Jerry."

"Well she really is stunning. I don't blame him. Hard to imagine that in twenty years she'll be built like a tank."

"They don't all, darling," she said. "Think of Sophia Loren."

"There was a time," his dad said, "when I did little else."

He watched the green Fiat drive off down the valley, coming back into view as it crossed each bridge, stirring brief dust behind it. He ordered another *orzata*, with two and a half hours to kill before his lunch date.

At death's door. Knock-knock-who's-there? The old man would probably just have fun with that if he told him. *Such a language!*

Was his mother afraid he would catch some contamination?

He wandered off at last, along the terrace. He revisited Clara's tomb, and the nest in the grass, but he just wanted time to pass. And tomorrow this would be nowhere.

Some boys had started a soccer game beside the river. He stood and watched. They were about twelve-years old, rowdy and sprinting about, ignoring the heat. "*Ciao,*" he called out, when he saw they had noticed him. "*Canadese!*"

They waved him in, shouting and laughing without interrupting the play, pointing out the side he must play on. He went easy at first because of his size, but some of them were quite miraculously skillful. His first competitive burst was foiled by a kid who didn't come up to his chest, dancing around like a terrier to steal the ball and then score. They cheered and jeered and whistled till it was easier to feel like an adult among them — clumsy and indulgent. He was exhausted in no time. But at least he had learned the Italian for "penalty kick" and "pass the ball" and "fuck off."

He got up to the Etrusco half an hour early, but they were there at their table, heads close together over a book.

She looked up, and immediately uncoiled from her chair and strode across the patio. She was fierce with urgency.

"Listen to me. You must forget about this eating together. He is too tired, though he will not say it. He did not sleep in the night."

"Alright., I'll leave."

"I will give you money to buy for yourself a meal somewhere else."

"It's okay, I said. Tell him I had to go with my parents."

She took hold of his forearm. A shiver went down to the pit of his stomach. "No," she said, "you must come for a little while. He has something to give you."

The teeth in her uncle's smile looked too big for his face. "Good," he said, "good. *Benvenuto!* Sit, sit, we have a chair for you." There was some mischief in his eyes as they moved from the boy to his niece and back again.

"And you have met Francesca," he said. "My angel. My guardian."

"Wasn't that your mother's name?"

The girl broke in: "My *piccola nonna.* She was one funky dame. I love her completely." Her right hand touched her uncle's brow, then his arm. She seemed unable to stop touching him. And he took her hand in his and raised it to his lips. Then held it against his cheek.

"I have been at work," he smiled. "I have this for you." He held out a small sheet of paper in his other hand. "It is a poem that I made, discovered I should say, in translating a German philosopher. A man many many people despise, and a man who feared death terribly. But he is still a great man, I believe. So, there — for you! An English translation of my Italian translation."

The writing sloped boldly forward in purple ink, the 'g's, 'y's and 'f's with jaunty underscrolls:

Man puts the longest distances behind him
In the shortest time. He sets the greatest distances
Behind himself, and thus sets everything
Before himself at the shortest range,
and yet
The frantic abolition of all distances
Achieves no closeness.

"Thank you," the boy said.

"As I said to you once before, I believe: No need for you to understand now, just please do not forget. And I think you will especially keep this as a momento of my Francesca, who wrote it out for you, because alas my hand-writing is becoming a mystery, even to myself."

The girl drew back her hand and swept it up through her hair. Her smile seemed completely open now, and as she rose from the table she saw the boy gazing into her dress and seemed, if amused, not offended. She actually brushed her fingers along his shoulders as she passed.

He folded the paper carefully, and unbuckled the binocular case. Its old leather breath was tinged with curry.

"So today you leave behind those earphones, but you have brought the empty case. It has found a new use?"

The boy laughed. "I just didn't want my Dad asking questions. I figured he'd be more likely to wonder if I *didn't* bring it."

"But you will have to explain this sooner or later."

"Later, I guess."

The girl slipped back into her seat. At once her hand went out to her uncle's and then began stroking his sleeve.

"Ah, Francesca. For the miserly sum, for the pittance I give to her, she is everything to me here."

Her hand slid up to his shoulder. "He pays my studies at university," she said. "Don't listen to him."

The waiter was there, with drinks for them all. The old man asked him a question, then started to speak rapidly, but the girl waved her hand between them: "No, no, *no!*" The waiter hesitated; the girl shooed him away

"There is no arguing with her," the old man's exasperation was more real than he pretended. "She will march me back to my bed, and spoil all our entertainment." More gently, he said: "It is discourteous, Francesca, you know this, to invite a guest —"

"It's okay," the boy said.

She murmured something in Italian. Her eyes were stern, she looked suddenly much older, more heavy of feature. The woman she would become, perhaps.

"*Va bene.* But first I have something to show you both."

He reached beneath the rug on his knees, and with some effort — pushing his body sideways in the chair with his free hand — worked something free from a pocket.

"Now," he said, "I will show you." He held up a watch, the kind people have to pull out to consult.

"This belonged to *my* grandfather," he said. "It was never of the best quality, yet it seems determined to limp out its time with me.

"But now I will tell you a story — concerning that battle," he looked up at the boy, "we were discussing yesterday. Yes I have told Francesca about your grandfather.

"So, as I told you, it ended up at the monastery. And on the last day, I was with three others, we had a machine gun, we were sheltering behind a — no I cannot recall the English word, the wall that holds up a wall, no matter, it was on the side of a chapel.

"Yes, of course it is terrible to think of the house of God as a battleground, terrible to think of the beautiful things, the history, the prayers, the memories, etcetera. etcetera. But what were we to do? We remembered Thermopylae, we remembered Horatius at the bridge, we were young men who would die to the last man. That is glory, yes?

"Suddenly, there was a tank — it was late in the day — there was a tank not 50 paces from us, and when it fired — darkness."

His niece was motioning him to be calm.

"*Sto bene. Non sono eccitato.*

"*Ecco.* They were not sure if I would live, and when I woke up they were not sure if I would walk."

The boy's eyes imagined the legs under that rug.

"No, no," the man shook his head. "I recovered fully, in the flesh that is to say. This is another disease, of old age — a weary heart, weary blood.

"But you wonder where this story is wending. All right. I had two, three operations and then, is maybe a year later and the war is all finished, and they 'check me over' at the big hospital in Ravenna. They x-ray my legs, they x-ray my back, then they x-ray my head — and this is what they find."

He turned the watch in his hands, trying to get enough purchase to open it. "*Patetico,*" he sighed. "You help me, Francesca."

The watch sprang open in her fingers. The dial was yellowed, the glass almost opaque. But, "No," he whispered, "*Il dietro. Apri la parte posteriore.*" She found a groove for her fingernail, and the back of the watch was a separate door. A fold of blue cloth fell onto the table. He gestured for her to give it to him.

"Now this," he said, "they extracted from the edge of my brain."

He laid his hand out in front of them. There was a dark piece of glass on the cloth. "Look," he said, "hold it to the light." The girl took it, and held it to her eye. She gasped. "*E l'occhio della Vergine,*" she muttered, and crossed herself, her fingers touching on each of her breasts. She slipped the thing back, and crossed herself again.

The old man nodded: "Now you." It was no bigger than the pottery shard from Francesca's lair. The boy turned in his chair to see the light through it. "Francesca thinks it comes from the Mother of God, but I think more likely a little saint, or who knows — a shepherd." The fragment was an eye, almost complete; even the eyebrow hairs were delicately brushed in. The iris was pale blue. The sun must be throwing the picture onto his face.

"I have to suppose that the tank shattered some windows, as well as my two comrades."

"And it was in your brain?"

"So they told me."

The boy dropped the little eye onto the outstretched palm. At that moment he felt stronger, older even, than Francesca.

The frail hand pushed itself further across the table towards him.

He's going to give it to me, he thought. He's going to give it to me, and I'll keep it in my bedroom with the owl's skull and the gold nugget and the shark's tooth.

He glanced with a sort of triumph at the girl, but whatever she was thinking, her eyes were fixed on her uncle.

"I would like you to tell me about your grandmother." The eye on the outstretched hand was suddenly a bribe.

"Tell me, was she, as they say, 'faithful to the memory' of her husband?"

What did he want? "She got married again, after a while. She had two more kids, and then they divorced when the kids had left home."

"But your grandfather's photograph, you said, was on her piano."

"Well sure. It was always there."

"Ah, *bene* . . . I like to think of a house with a piano. And does your grandmother play?"

"Yeah, she's good. So's my dad."

"And the piano, does it stand near a window?"

The girl was caressing her uncle's arm again. But the sight of those teeth in the painful smile, and the green eyes' intense interest . . . No the old guy couldn't help how he looked.

"It's right *in* a window. What's its face, a bay window?"

"Ahh," said the old man, "Francesca — imagine.

"And can you tell me what your grandmother sees when she plays her piano and looks out from her bay window?"

This was too weird. "The main thing she sees is a lilac tree. She planted it the day my sister was born. It's twenty three years old."

"That is courage, my young friend. It is courage and — *elegance*, and faith."

"I guess so."

"Now," he laboured to sit up and lean forward. His niece tried to restrain him, but he waved her off. "I shall ask you, and trust you, to be my Hermes, my messenger between worlds. Will you do that for me?"

"I'm not sure what you mean."

"I would like you to take this — relic, and give it to your grandmother. I would ask you to tell her the whole truth about those binoculars, and to give her my gift, and to tell her the truth about that also. I believe she will understand." He had spoken with great deliberation. Now the hand began to slip back across the table. "Take it, please."

The boy did take it. He folded the cloth around it again, and opened his binocular case. And then, on an impulse:

"Look, I found this yesterday. It's not very impressive, but I guess it's really old. Here, it's for you." The old man had shrunk right back in his chair. The boy had to get up, and open one of the hands, folded on the rug. The shard of pottery lay grey upon the parchment skin; the zigzag lines had a sudden violence to them.

"*Then 'twas the Roman, now 'tis I.* Have you encountered that poem yet, in your studies . . . ? Ah, you are very kind," and he inverted his hand, pressing the fragment back into the boy's palm. "You are very kind, but I must not accept. All I have left to do is to give. But I thank you, I thank you — it will not be forgotten."

The boy turned to Francesca: "Maybe you'd like it."

"Me? I would only lose it! But I thank you too."

The old man was breathing through his nose. It was a scary sound, convulsive and animal. The girl moved round behind the wheelchair, and started massaging her uncle's shoulder and chest, resting her chin very lightly on his brow. "Time for you to go," she said.

"I have not cared very much for my body." It sounded like an announcement, the voice more high-pitched than before, but speaking seemed to make the breath come more gently, and the old man ignored his niece's shushing whispers. "Since my Lydia died, I have devoted myself entirely to the life of the mind. And Lydia would laugh to hear me say that — she would say that nothing has changed!" He leaned back, smiling up at Francesca: "I am not without memories, though." She kissed his brow, a slow kiss with those wonderful, full lips. Her hands did not stop for a moment their slow massage.

"My body shall leave me soon." He looked back at the boy; there was mischief again in his eyes. "I frighten you I know. I am sorry for that."

"You don't frighten me. You frightened my mother."

"Imagine that. You must greet her from me, with respect. A sensitive lady." He closed his eyes. "Yes my body shall leave me — not so soon as you think: Francesca understands. Not so soon, but soon. At the moment I have no intention of accompanying it."

Softly, the girl spoke the boy's thoughts, though her tone was more playful than anything, and spoken in English: "But where will that leave you?"

"It is perhaps as futile to speculate on that point, as to surrender." His eyes were still shut. The girl motioned with her head for the boy to leave.

He buckled the binocular case. And stood up. "Well. *arrivaderci*," he said. One hand lifted fractionally from the rug. The girl flashed him a quick smile: "*Si —* bye."

He turned at the top of the stairs and watched. Her hands pushed steadily on the old chest and shoulders, and she was crooning, singing under her breath, with a smile that seemed quite unconcerned with sickness. Her face, and her movements, reminded him of his mother at the sink and then, even more, of his grandmother kneading bread at the end of her long table.

She looked up and saw him there and looked down again. But a few seconds later, she moved her hands to her uncle's forearms, and looked steadily into the boy's face, still kneading, still crooning, but looking . . .

Twelve years would pass, and he would be walking home through the lanes of a western city in the first miraculous haze of fatherhood, before he remembered that moment in Tuscany. He did not at once recall the girl's name, but her face was suddenly vivid in the prairie dawn, leaning towards him over her uncle's bowed head, and he understood, or felt that he did, what her eyes had been trying to tell him.

prelude

Brother Dael came to me one April morning in Connemara when the larks were all at once singing, the blackthorns were in bloom and, whether or not God was in his heaven, all seemed right with the world.

I visualised him stepping out into the sunlight, from a little stone hut like the ones on the edge of our townland, and casting his merry shadow, with its arms outstretched in benediction, upon the waking earth.

He seemed like the spirit of Spring, but he was unmistakeably a friar too.

He grew upon me as I started to write for him. This gentle, innocent old man who doesn't realise that he is dead and who — if he did realise it — would be mildly astonished and confirmed in his sense of wonder.

I think I was engaged in inventing a saint. (A thought that would make him laugh.) A total heretic too, of course, but then all the best saints are.

We seem more likely today to credit saintliness to people involved in good works than to those who follow the contemplative life. For me, though, contemplatives — along with poets, composers, artists and other prayer-makers — are our saving grace even though in Auden's phrase, they "make nothing happen." If there's a day of judgement we may find out the truth of that.

Who knows, William Blake may have seen things more clearly:

The hermit's prayer and the widow's tear
Alone can free the world from fear.

Besides, Brother Dael has earned his hermitage, and his optimism, after suffering through the relentless horrors of the Thirty Years War and Cromwell's rape of Ireland. (The story is set in the 1650s — one of the first rhymes I ever learned was In sixteen hundred and fifty eight Oliver Cromwell became The Late — so the potatoes are not quite an anachronism.)

The old man has won through to a second innocence (some might say a second childhood, though I'm not sure if you can accuse a ghost of senility). He inhabits a world of wonder (which Creation is, of course, if you really attend to it), the place from which Meister Eckhart wrote: The eye we see God through is the eye through which he sees us.

It's a great way to sum up a life, I think — to end and begin with a celebration of the Creation, all of its creatures, from the winter wrens and the seed-hoard, to the devils of sin and temptation, to human beings of every behaviour.

Unrealistic? That's how saints become saints.

When you write from inside a character's mind you cannot give explanations of things he or she takes for granted, but I realise that some of the historical or folkloric allusions in this story may intrigue or irritate some readers.

So there's a page of notes at the very end of this book to help clarify things. Just one note, here, in advance: "the Little Flower" is Francis of Assisi; "the Little Dove" is Columcille (Columba to the non-Celtic world). None of the actions or words attributed to these saints is my invention.

BROTHER DAEL'S NEW YEAR

So winter was changed to mud. It was past remembering. To save his sandals ruin he splashed barefoot
along the back of his house toward the well-path. The
simple air. He stood and breathed, eyes closed, as if it
were his first breath ever. Yes. The heart's discipline had
brought him out into the light again. He moved on,
hands held loosely out from his sides, open to the day.
The mud and the water were too cold for any feeling: his
foot gashed off a hidden stone and his mind must invent
the small pain. He picked his robe's hem clear of the
ankle-depth of staining ooze; the high bog seemed to
have flowed over with the melting snow and smeared his
careful half-acre brown and black.

No matter, all around he could hear the world waking
to water: freshets in every coombe, the brookflood inching up by his gate, the moss-rocks drenched with the sliding abundance. Ice was a clean, cold memory. A still
memory. The past remembering. His bones cramped in
the restless shifts of Spring.

When the sun struggled up it raised mist from the wet-
lands and the shore. And the mists held back the sun.
And so it would go for a week, he supposed. The mists
lolled on the water — you would not say that they rose or
fell — and they shifted nowhere. Air was a grey element,
moulding the lost earth. Sky was a supposition.

Nothing outside himself moved. The air closed out all
sounds but the water and his footfalls, which were water
too. But along the drowned path the mist came fawning
and tumbling towards him. He petted it, he laughed and
soothed, stroking its loose manes, and it closed around
him and followed as he climbed the rough steps worn in
the Saint's rock.

Now he was clear of the water, the mist floundered in
the low blackthorn thicket and the outer branches wore
its fleece like rags and pennants. He skirted the thorns
and eased himself up onto the eggspeckle throne of granite, unconscious of the chill or the damp stone. He bent
forward, murmuring, indulging but insisting. The mist lay
down for a little space around him and he could see,
through a veil, the bay faintly below. The ice had parted
into floes of all sizes, there were creeks and currents of
dark water angling between the green and the grey. Such
green: winter's sea-emerald. He imagined, if he did not
see, a black boat jockeying through the serried ice-plates
towards his island. He was content.

He looked down upon his rooftop. The corbelled bee-
hive of a home, shape of an upturned boat, a tent of
stones that had earned, through the centuries, accept-
ance back into the land it had been quarried from.
Somewhere in the world's morning when the Saints had
toiled. The curving houseflank was patterned and
scabbed with lichens; so were the thorn-boughs, and the

rock seat he was perched on now. His eyes lost a shade of focus, straining for that shape in the moss-patterns which was trying to surface through the stones of his house. A figure be almost remembered. He could not grasp it. No matter.

Nothing mattered very much. His fingers lay lightly upon the stone wings of the Saint's throne and he gazed with detached fondness at the neat stone cell where he had passed his winter. The other clachans along the cliff were shelters for sheep only; so had his been until last Spring, when Micháel McCahil had hung the rough door of wreck-timbers for him. It opened inwards and the fisherman had rolled a big stone inside for a stop against the wind. His bed had been soft, dry generations of sheeps' dung. Yes, he had spent all winter there, alone. Except for his little friends.

Memories sifted down like the ashes upon his hearth. Micháel — *We don't choose to come over here too often. Only for the minding of the sheep.* Who must take their chances, like a hedge-priest, for the winter. Micháel, grim and generous, his ferryman last Spring when the others had looked away, across to the Saint's isle. Who had taken without remark his last small coin, a clipped *stater* that had travelled more roads and paid for more sins than he could dream of. Ah, Micháel knew the discipline of the will: danger meant nothing to him, only for his family. The giver of seed, too, and sardonic counsel — *You'll be in need against the solitude . . . I'll find you a dog.* But a pup would be chasing the sheep and breaking the stillness. He could turn to the flock and to the wild things for company . . .

The memories merged with the mist and were forgotten. He was content.

The well was the heart of this time and place. The blackthorns girdled it, spreading their harsh net over its lips, yet they were touched already by Grace. Before the world came fully alive, out of the bitter spite of the wind from Thule white flowers sprang. They clutched the hilts of the long thorns before the leaf buds so much as relaxed. The wind, he divined, was two days dead — the flowers, like barnacles, watched for the new tide.

At once he remembered the Wren's death. And the end of patience — the cock bird strutting upon the hearth and the host of little visitors who followed, clamouring and unruly, to thread his vigil against Winter's dead heart.

There could never have been such a winter. He had been lost — loneliness had gripped him as the cold could not. He fingered the rim of a lichen cockade; the mist shifted and crept closer, on its belly. The bay was swallowed again, his house back was the one solid thing below — black like a whale's hump in the grey sea. But he could fathom those stones now, could riddle the ash-heap for the Wren's death and the half-remembered months.

They had come each evening, packing a crevice of the corbells in his back wall, sharing each other's warmth. Winter wrens. They had stirred and chuckled in the night, scraping in the stones; once he had let the fire die they were his only company. Out of a shadow sleep he had woken, summoned, and the Wrens were still. That was Fear, that was the ice-locks clamping on the house and, as the earth stopped, the stone vault of his home was a sudden, descending tunnel of loneliness. But in that instant the cock bird had declared itself on his hearth, chest puffed and ember-red, scratching stiff-legged and impatient so that the ash-flakes flew out around it, claiming its kingdom. The Robin had found his way in where no draught could, and out through his legs came swarming the procession of friends.

So fear was changed to laughter. He had teased them from the start, as they filled his cell with warmth and mischief and that almost smothering musty taint, as if he had tumbled, headlong and laughing, into a nest of mice. They squealed and squirmed about him and he named them the Wren Boys, mocking, for their scuttling mummery. They had hunted the Wren and were come in their guises for his tribute. But the ferryman had the last of his silver, so they played for his Soul. He laughed aloud at the memory, and the sound broke out, astonishing, into the air around the Saint's throne where he sat. He waited in the echo, wishing the light would recede for a while and let him back among the companions. For he missed them — they had cheered him, pitting their sweet monstrosities against the discipline of his old heart.

But they were gone now, the temptations — the shy, grotesque wild creatures come to be gentled, with their snouts and bat's ears and pearly fangs, and each so eager to loll and display the little wet hell-mouths, pink wounds in the coarse growth of their fur. They had clamoured so for his attention — when he inclined to one of them another would whimper and insist, hooking and tugging at his robe with its black claws while the rest swarmed over his shoulders, whispering their poor, vile litanies, hopefully at his ears. If they stank, up close, of fear and glee and excrement, he loved them still — most of all the little blind one who stood his ground till the house fell silent, staring up with ice-capped blue eyes, the most nearly human, an absurd manikin, stubbornly pouting like a mutinous boy. For whom at last he himself had gathered them all in a half-circle and taught them to sing for their brother, with hushed voices, the cataracts of pride. It was a discipline of the heart.

Heresy was a cruel, draughty word, snake-eyed, relentless. Its syllables were ruled between straight lines, spoken through bars. He had crossed half Europe to be free of it, discarding the disciplines of mind and will like gay rags into mountain updraughts, down forest trails, upon hedges and dykes. Stepping lighter, despite the world, as he neared the West, reciting each dawn the text of the Little Flower — *So much desire in these days for wisdom and learning, Happiness to him who for God's sake discovers ignorance.* The second phrase went to an air, full of grace-notes and runs, he had heard a young girl sing by the Rhine, herding her geese. He came to sing it as he went. The paths to the sea did not go in straight lines, they followed the whims of the Creation. Bless them, for all their devious snares they had brought him in hope to the low countries, and thence into the West.

Tempted by Hope? Oh guilty through and through. As if Hope were the great Damnation. Europe had thinned into massacre and plague, with hogs rooting in the choked ditches and the smoke of policy rolling across the earth. The steel helmets surveyed the heart and drew straight lines with swordpoints and the articles of faith, but there was joy and energy to confound them. To include them, even — the woodbine embracing the stake. The eyes of heaven approved. Yes, the birds saw things with a more loving eye. Surely the heart was a bird, one truth in the books, and the cage was only ribs of sunlight at last.

If he had lived in the Saint's time he would have ruled six lines, like a music stave, and written the words, if the words had been thought then, *The second death will do them no harm*; he would have written, besides, the reproof of the Shepherd, come down through the Lion's mouth — *He is not the god of the dead but the god of the living, ye therefore do greatly err.* And then he would marry the disciplines of hand and eye to embroider the straight text with the brambling joy that was the words' flesh — writhing beasts and contorted men, the rebellious harmonies of slaughter and pestilence, the earthbound riot, breaking out of the bars of dark rule into the sunlight of praise. And colour, oh blessed be colour in this grey scape. But he had shed those disciplines too, and besides, the Saint's age was past remembering except in this last, rocky place.

The vision of colours played across the mist's skin, around the house walls. Outside himself, he wondered at the scales of memory, coiling back into forgetfulness at the least touch. The day was no further advanced, the sky was still closed. He willed his feet to the Saint's well among the thorns and knelt to look down through the rock. Here there was life abundant — maidenhair ferns clustered along the courses of stone: spring green, untouched by the winter. Five feet below was a still brightness of light with nothing between it and the grey day it reflected. Just so the Saint, when he laboured on the house, must have kneeled and watched in the first days and left no image, alas, looking back from the deep water. There was a trout down there, to keep the well sweet, he had glimpsed it, bullheaded, when Micháel had brought him here last Spring. Never since. It had always been there, the fisherman said, placed there he supposed, grinning, by the Saint himself. The trout, ageless hermit, bright spirit in darkness from the Saint's careful hands — in the Summer had come a morning hymn to the guardian of the well and continuance — *Flesh of the holy fish under the stone, Flesh of the holy fish under the dawn.* Who knew the source of these sacraments, the simple canticles which came unbidden? He had wondered. That was the time when he felt that the Saint haunted the place still though his bones, as everyone knew, lay in Hibernia.

The Saint's name, duly reverenced, became a prayer, habitually murmured. It reached all the presences here. Not that the Saint had been a companion exactly, not like his little troop of deceivers; rather that the shadow thrown out behind him by the lamp upon his wall had come to seem another's, and his own skin had been, for a spell, unfamiliar. Then, at times, the man he was had seemed past remembering, absorbed in the stones and the echoes of prayer. The first time that happened he had actually been in dread — the foolishness! — for the shadow had whisked up from the floor like a spider of black down, too light for scuttling, not raising a breath in the warm hearth or stirring a crumb of the sheep-dung pallet. He had caught it at his eye's corner, during Compline, at the heart of an *Ave*, and his heart had checked, as if the Father of Lies had come visiting with nightfall. But that had been one with the presences and the scamperings in the old house, calmed soon enough by the heart's discipline, almost past remembering.

Sweet water and ferns and the blossoming thorn. The well was a miracle above all things in this place — sunk in the rock at the island's highest point. From its lip in the Summer you could see unhindered the world curving over all below you — the whale-path of the Navigator, on to Hy Brasil and the Blessed Isles; the goosetrail north towards Thule, where the Little Dove had set out upon exile; and the long, curving route of the scallop-shells, down into Biscayne and the spires of Santiago. Only the hills to the east, on the mainland that was itself a small island, the last but one, broke into the sky. The widening Pale — beyond the hills the steel helmets and the measured curse of Europe.

But at this still, high point the holy fish swam and the water never failed. And he had imagined the Father of Lies! Yet the Little Flower had known this too — *He is in the water we drink, the bread we eat, the bed we lie down in.* And then the sweet heretic, say what they will, had urged the true charity upon his sisters — *Kiss Satan's tormented countenance, so that his first, radiant face may be restored to him.*

The Saint, who had made this well and raised their home, must have learned this too. Yes, that Satan was in the flower, under the stone, in the branches of the fruit tree. Ferdia's Well they called it, in the townlands round the bay, yet — *We do not choose to come over here too often.* Ferdia had left, called north by the Little Dove who turned his back upon Ireland. Who knew Satan too, yet feared the sound of an axe in the groves of Derry worse than all the fires of Hell. Who had sent Ferdia to death, buried beneath the church floor of Hy for three days, to learn the truth. When they unearthed him he called out, *Hell is nothing like they've painted it!* and *Earth,* cried the Little Dove in terror, *earth upon Ferdia!*

That half-fledged novice Findbarr Doog, newly Brother Albanus, had told him that story, homesick and newly arrived at Bobbio, and he had failed to reprove him, though it was the very stuff his learning had taught him to censure. It was the sound of the old language, perhaps — its uncouthness and vague colloquial energy, after the Latin discipline of their foundation. That, and the uncle-love that came over him as he took the boy's arm, along the sun-sharp terrace into the library, and placed his hand on the old book. The colours, bald as a whore's enamelled gear, seemed to catch fire from the sun in the long dark room. And the boy's eyes too. The body and face of youth, and the innocence of that island which Europe had left behind. That child had turned him perhaps towards the words of the Little Flower — it had started there, surely. Now, free of Europe in this first and last place, and with Ferdia's spirit before him, he had learnt, like a holy fool, to believe.

Therefore the shoremen went in fearful love of the Saints, as though the Saints were faeries. The good folk. And they were not far wrong, perhaps. Besides, the new race of "fathers", for all their simple courage, shared that fear. The Saints first, then his own kind, scattered like books throughout Europe, and at last the hedge-priests, flat-footed souls who could pass as peasants in these penal times and go unmolested. Who understood and taught by rote, drawing straight rules with their blunt fingers, blundering Latin into their native tongue, clutching the wheaten host like a fetish. That one in the village, when he had first arrived, at Hehir's croft, looking at him with distrustful calf's eyes and slab-lips pursed, filling the people with unease. That one would not choose to venture across to the Saint's Isle in the bay; he chose hearthside and company, and the glum reverence of his dispensation. He brought no hope — he dealt in dumb ritual and poor authority, balancing Hell against the Ascendancy. It was not the "ignorance" of the Flower or the Dove.

Did Pride, Mistress Pride stare him in the face, even now? That hedge-priest was at one with the people, while he, the exile, was an emblem out here, remote as the fonts of Rome, praying with the tricky shades of the Saints. No threat, but no kindred. Micháel McCahil at least understood, and watched him with a grim, apprising humour, as he might a wayward tup browsing thrift on the cliffs' edge. He had forgotten Micháel in this savage Atlantic winter, when the ice glazed the stones of his house and sealed him from the world, but Micháel would not have forgotten him. He would have glanced out, each afternoon across the locked bay, wondering how the Brother fared — and the sheep too in their stone shelters — sparing a thought as you would for the fortunes of a departed soul. Well, he had Micháel's respect at any rate, though the ferryman could never guess at the game he had played on the townland's behalf after the cold set in.

But Micháel was exceptional; in his way he cared and understood — his kindness was dour and unwhimsical, he had the will's clear discipline and that stood for hope in his small world. Micháel had foretold this winter from the bird flocks and the dogberries, and had made sure there was a good stock of fuel laid in with the food in the storeshed. He would be first across when the ice broke, might be on his way already. With Cormac, his eldest, no doubt — and there was a blessing in *his* future, for to him it had been given to find the bell, green and carbuncled, time-choked in the bog, as they had turned out turf, the three of them last May behind the well. The Saint's bell surely, hanging now, with its dripping clapper of ice, from a stake thrust into the corbells by the door.

He should ring it when the mists had drawn away. To tell them that Hope lived on the bay, that their troubles had wrestled with him, and spared them, while the shore ice cracked like cannon shots through the days of misrule. No hurry, though — the ice was retreating, the boat would thread the bay, and he would come, in good time, back to the people with bright words for the Spring.

The world held still. There were no sounds or smells, save in the ash-heap of memory; there was only the closed, reflective vision of the mist. No matter. In its own time the Creation would reawake. Part of him must still be held by winter. But he was awake — he rose and stood smiling among the thorns. A thin runnel of water came from the rock below his feet, an overflow from the unfailing well. A sheep lay with its muzzle in the tiny stream. It was long dead but even its eyes were intact, held by the cold, looking up at him like glazed yellow stones. It was waiting too. Spring, and the birds returning, would renew its dissolution. And the rest of the half-wild flock? Was he derelict in his duty — should he have looked out for the sheep as he had offered to Micháel? And the boatman had shrugged — *They must take their chances. As God wills.* He would think about it later. When he turned to look down again at his house the mist heaved up as if to play, but he stilled it with grave eyes. He was searching. Again that shape among the lichens was reaching towards him, rising through the stones. Some buried thing, he could not reach it. He remembered the Lady.

Oh memory. These dream wisps that came with their own life, unbidden. He had been in peril of forgetting her. Who had brought light when his second patience failed, when he could find no more songs and his little friends began to riot in his solitude. The house had seemed a maze suddenly, like the pattern of a key thrust into the heart of the glacial season, rusting upon him. And she had stood before him, showing the way clear, her face like the Lord's himself, simple and various as all the moods of the Creation resolved into a laugh to banish perplexity. His flock had known her, had scampered across to her, laughing and whispering up as she bent to them — the little flaunter most of all, peering out at the hem of her dress, rubbing like a cat against her white ankles. They all knew her, she belonged here, yet he himself had recognized her from a hundred distant places along both his paths — the Dove's Way east towards learning and ambition, the Flower Track back from Italy away from conviction and sanctuary.

She was the kind heart of famine. He had seen her face in Europe over and over, on the carrion plains and in the smouldering villages; on the wharf at La Caruña; among the refugees who choked the passes out of the Pale. And once, in the low countries, when the wagons receded and a last roof collapsed into the flames as the sparks flew up, she had crawled to him where he hid in the ditch, as if she knew he was there. Her eyes had looked through him towards the rank water, her mouth was a caving crust of blood, the flies fed on her breath. The red shadows of that night had clothed her looted nakedness, her hand had reached blindly into his face. Before he could help her to water she was gone; and now she had come in his need. Bride was her name here — the shorefolk would be hanging her rush cross under the thatch when the ice left. She had reached for his hand as he followed her footprints through the cold ashes on the hearth, and she had sent him on, with her blessing.

Fear nothing. The land beyond had been ashes, fine dust as though the hearth endured to the horizon. Eagle and wolf fled from the harrow as it traced straight furrows ahead of him. They screamed and circled around the plough, swooping at him, snapping at the tines. For this was Hell — which was the mind of a cruel man. That was all. And enough. The Little Dove had laughed at Froichan. Hugh O'Neill had danced *The Walls of Limerick* in Ireton's face; he himself, in that week, had smiled back at the Saxon lad who swung the knout at him. For they were beautiful, eagle and wolf, though they carried Hell within them. He called them to him, braiding the furrows with his reins, and their talons flayed his pride, their teeth splintered his sloth, his love and their energy flowed together. From where the bird circled, freed from its bars, there was harmony. Everyone sang, the dust had blossomed, and the Bride restored him to her white breast.

He went down with the water, singing the trout's canticle, towards the store-shed. The mist followed, slipping after him along the rocks, to jostle and flow about his waist. At the shed he found at last the shape that had been calling to him all morning from the stones of his house — it was figured in the weathered grain of the pinewood door. A man lying in a space confined. Legs bent, knees together, leaning. Arms bent, hands clasped before the inclining chest. A face with staring eyes and mouth framed as if to whistle. The little man might be crouching, begging, or at prayer — might have fallen over in mid-prayer and lain still. No, looked at another way the figure seemed poised to leap, or dive or spring. But was held in that stillness as though enclosed in a womb. The huge black pupils and the whistling port of the mouth peered out at the world.

If he had been the Saint at his vellum, that figure should have bounded across the staves. The little frog man. With his hand at the wooden door-latch he turned and peered through the mist. His house was only a bulking shadow. He became the frog man, he willed himself into that face. He made a whistle for the mouth — a soft

231

rush of air, growing — and gestured inland with his left arm the direction he spelled.

With the whistle came the sea-wind, over the hill at his back, and blew along his arm towards the twelve hills. The mist recoiled and parted like a wave so that his hand pushed clear through: first the bay, then the flat miles of bog and stonecrop. He waved his arm to brush it all away and the wind tore in on a long front. The drenched thatch trembled above him as he turned into the shed's darkness, knowing that when he stepped out again the snow-topped peaks would be clear to his view.

From Spring he stepped into the dust of Fall. And at once smell came back to the earth. The breath of the stacked turf, the patience of salt, the apple-sweet freshness of good keeping; and with these, new memories. At October's end, with Micháel and young Cormac, he had stacked all the stores and seed from his land, and some of their giving, safe from the damp and the wreck-rats. He had not imagined leaving them these long months, but so it had been. Strange, too, that with grain and potatoes there in the bins he had not come for them in the winter, and it so cold and famished. They would have made a comfort of the Christ's Tide too, and cheered his companions. Ah no. There was no knowing after all, it was past remembering. He would think about it later.

But how they had laboured at this little shed! The three of them, straddling the low walls, with armfuls of reeds from the bog side to lay across the rough scaffold of hazel wands. The sheep-bitten wands, springing from the rock cracks all over his island, the only straight lines, perhaps, that the Creation tolerated. And through them the strong arms of Cormac, the massive but deft fingers of his father, threaded the pliant stems. And himself helping, a clumsy novice delighting in the new skills and the industry, laughing, it seemed to him now, through the whole joyous week. Yes, he'd found strength, he had learned endurance along the Flower Track, and he found a child's pride in their respect. Why, that fellowship and labour was prayer itself, threading the staves. But then they had looked at him in a new way after he had stripped to the waist to work with them and they had seen his back. The harrow-lines, the grid of that lashing outside Limerick. When he had reeled from the gallows, weaving from exhaustion and pain across the bright field, while the ranks of boys laid on. Boys they had been, like Cormac but dulled by false disciplines, and he had fastened on the eyes of one youngster and smiled as the lash fell. That remained to him, as the essence of the pain. Well, enough of that. And these good people had brought an old fish-net to hold down the thatch, a last grid upon their labour of love, weighted by stones. And see, it had survived the storms of winter.

Now, but he would need light. He carried no knuckle of hot turf to kindle the oil wick by the door. No, for there had been no fire when he left his house. Fire he could remember only as a fallen cone of sifted, feathery grey, with sand-layers, fine as bone ash. There had been no fire all that time, no — he had never stepped out after the snow, never rolled back the stone and ventured to the turf pile. That could have meant warmth and light, dancing on the cold walls. Perhaps it would have been wiser. He would think about it later. But the light — *Little Bride, little Bride,* he murmured, *spare me this trouble.* Squinting towards the corners, tented in shadows. *Little fire-sister, come to my hand.* Would the barley be free from the mildew still? There was no knowing without light. She would be a young child, if you named her one. Or a crone, laughing. *Little one, little one, at my need* . . . The smokey flame cleared lazily and the light crept up the limewashed walls, over the wooden bins canted upon their stones, up to the dry scraws below the thatch, shaking slightly from the wind beyond.

The lamp sat in a recess by the door and he moved towards his shadow, genuflecting familiarly to Ferdia's precedence. His robe loomed, shapeless, angling sharply at the roof. It was comforting in this half-lit old shieling, breathing patience, and yet exciting too. He loved shelters — shelter from the wind, from rain, from sun, from anything in the world when you could duck into shade for a spell and hear the rumour of strong things safe above your head. Weren't walls and a roof a great thought for a man to have had?

His lean old fingers intrigued him. He paused to watch them, so delicately reaching under the first bin's lip and then with an unhurried strength pull out the headboard. Peas it was, yellow in the lamp-light but green to his mind. Running through his hands, dry as should be — *oh white, veiny flowers, little archways of thorns, and strong green whips to cling with.* And the tight pearls of barley — *Field of silk,* the headboard flew, *the wind-friend, earth-wave, ale-oh!* He felt like dancing to the year ahead. The seed-potatoes, from Micháel. He clapped his hands together. And they knew, look, they were clustering up to his bent face: pale, eager stalks.

The shed was stacked with promise, all safe. *Oh Bride and Christ and Flowering Thorn* he called in happiness *let us have out the Sun again!* He stepped to the door and, pulling it wide, flung out the lamp at the sky to gild the twelve peaks and lie with passion on the water's breast.

He stood pierced with sound and taste, giddy with light. It was almost the light of Italy, Assisi light, clear and possible, linking heaven and earth. Now all that was past remembering yielded to the things he knew by heart. The final sweet discipline. From his house came the summons of the Saint's bell, calling down the wind to the waiting people. The flatlands over the bay danced with colour and light: so he had seen the world after Limerick, when he'd run between ranks of steel helmets, wavering with confusion in the drunkenness of pain, as the Dove in him died and flew round and between the standards and then up, curving around the church spires, watching the dance in sunlight on the radiant field below. *Fear nothing* chanted the bell.

He was eager now, to be busy at last — hurrying into the clear day, as old and agile as the song in his throat. Where to begin? There was no knowing after all. He would think about it later. But all the time, and good time, lay around him. He blessed the holy winter, he sang, he laughed like a child.

There was the year's first bird a curlew up from the shore. *The goat-bird, good; the dawn-waker, yes. And soon the swallow and the cuckoo too, and the shiny chough in my chimney!* He went to his house, black and gleaming now from the wet and the light. He reached to touch the stones, while the bell, intermittently, called. The miraculous, level courses of flat stones, curving over so that the walls became the roof, were an art from the Saint's time, permanent as the parent rocks, past remembering. Though the Wrens had died, life of all kinds lingered in the crevices. Tufts of thrift, glassworts, and sleeping miniature forests of moss. Snailshells packed one cavity, a furled companionship in limbo, dreaming, assured of release.

The horn-coloured shells were sealed, the delicate purple and umber bands were muted until light and life, from within and without, should infuse them. Were we all born sealed in a caul, and the Creation a vague light and song beyond the membrane, till the light broke savagely in and the bird was freed? A small husk, shaped like a date's pit, clung on the lee side of one stone: a tortoise-shell butterfly hung there in limbo while the sun crept round the house.

The wind, accomplished, was dropping. And now, voices from the path below the cliff. Well, good, good, they were all good people here. Micháel, he would wager. Micháel and young Cormac come over the water to wish him "Good Year". He would meet them.

He stopped by the drystone wall, smiling over the blonde twigs of the waking fuschia tangle, his arms spread in his wide, flapping sleeves and his old face alive and smiling with simple courtesy. "Micháel McCahil it is *good* to see you." Though they passed him indifferently at the gate, he could not care. "They do not see me," he laughed, and hurried after them.

And "They need not be so *solemn*," as they looked grimly at each other and back to the silent clachan. Micháel in his black boots and green stained hill-cloak; Cormac in a new weave of russet brown. "A good mother," he thought, "she provides well for them. And that sack the boy has — a gift for me, surely." And he wanted and wanted to peep into it without their knowing.

Micháel moved slowly to the door, scowling at the flooded threshold. He tried the door. It held. "Let *me*, let *me*," the old man chided. He shrugged apologetically at the sky; they should not *worry* so, but there it was. The door gave to the boatman's shoulder, the boulder grated back in the darkness. "Stay you here," he said curtly to his son. He was gone a minute or so. The old man watched a whole flock of curlews swing across the bog — nine, eleven — fourteen of them. Such a crowd. Soon they would be pairing.

The fisherman came out and shook his head. "Ach, before Christmas, I'd say." He spat, and breathed in the Spring air deeply. "We'll come back tomorrow with your uncle and some others — the priest if he's willing — twill be time enough."

They waded on towards the shed. Cormac stuck close by his father's side, looking back over his shoulder. The bell sounded once more. He followed them: "You should understand; I have great news for you." But if they would not listen, it was still true. Sad they should walk so heavily, but it would come true for them most of all. *Whoever plants the seed,* he thought, *shall bless this Summer.*

Yes, that was right. "Oh merry angels," he told the guardian hills, "isn't this a Springtime to have lived for?"

♈ ♈ ♈

prelude

My original note on this last, title story was very brief. It said little more than, "This is a true story, though you may choose to read it as fiction."

But that was avoiding the issue.

We tell stories differently, depending on whether they're invented or remembered. One creates life, the other reports on it.

And you cannot pretend they're the same.

"A Traveller Came By" doesn't work as a "ghost story", Ghost stories are creepy. (A friend of mine had to take *The Turn Of The Screw* out into the middle of a field on a summer's afternoon to finish it, she was so scared.)

The experience I'm dealing with here wasn't creepy at all.

I think I resisted calling this a memoir out of shyness.

People are so hungry for miracles, and I don't want to seem to be feeding that hunger.

A winter wren is a far greater miracle than a ghost. So is a lynx, a salmon, an autumn crocus, the threshold where an apple tree's bark parts the earth.

Catching sight of a mountain bluebird — a tremor of light, more blue than bird, across a dark shelterbelt of pines — my friend Paddy O'Rourke said, "That's as close to seeing an angel as we'll come in this life."

But in a society where most people don't know what phase the moon is in, the miracles are shrouded (or diminished by the reductive aspect of science).

A ghost came to see me. He played a joke on me. And the more that joke echoes in my mind, the more interesting I find it.

A memoir, then, to end this book: a low-key, cheerful memoir as the tale of a joke should be.

The title is a line from William Blake's *Never Seek To Tell Thy Love.*

A TRAVELLER CAME BY

About five days after he died, out on the Coast, Freddy came knocking at my door. He was standing there in the darkness, with the screen held open, and it took me a moment to know him. "I don't believe it," I said, and I found his name on my tongue. "How in Hell did you track me down here?"

I hadn't seen him for fifteen years maybe, though I'd heard the stories, and I'd spent that time in two countries, three provinces, more homes than I'd care to count.

He put his finger to his lips and slipped past me into the house, shimmying away from my hesitant impulse to hug him. "Don't tell anyone I was here," he murmured, and then stepped into my living room. He looked about him and nodded slowly, folding his arms. "You always find a home," he said, more to the room than to me.

And it's true — if that's what he meant — that I've learned to turn a new space into mine very quickly. A roof, four walls, hot running water: bare, luxurious necessity, decked out with my touchstones and tokens of memory, with the pictures and masks and statuettes, the prayer rugs and hangings, which this nomad has gathered and hung onto. In the two months I'd been here the little house had taken on the blend of lair and study which makes me at home.

And now, like the breathing past, his name and features distilled from the misty Pacific islands where I had come to know him, this thick-shouldered figure stood in my living room, a thousand miles from the Coast, and seemed to take stock of my life.

I was surprised, and touched I guess, that he had remembered me. But there it is — I remember people, why should I expect them to forget me? And I do confess, I was wondering, too, *What does he want?* Why would he be here, down near the border, at the edge of the Cypress Hills? I'd never had trouble with Freddy, but his name spelled trouble to everybody who knew him.

He might want money; he might need somewhere to hide.

"So where are you heading?" I asked. "Which way are you going?" Whatever the case, he'd made a detour fifty miles south of the trans-Canada, on dirt roads mostly, to find this small town in its river-snake valley. Or had he come up from the States?

He turned, and his forefinger rose to his lips again: "Don't tell anyone I was here."

"You said that already," I laughed. "There's no one to tell, around here."

But he still didn't answer. There was something about his manner, something melodramatic and smug, as if he might twirl a cloak around him: *But soft, we are observed!* Yes, smug, as though he were fondling a secret.

"You want a drink?" I asked. " — or tea, coffee?"

"Tea's always good," and he filled his strong chest with air, breathing deliberately in through his nose, as I always remember him doing. He looked me up and down, with that knowing, nodding assessment of his, and his eyes passed over my shoulder to a mask that hung at the doorway. A Kwakiutl dance mask, *Bukwus* the Wild Man, one of my real treasures. He gave a small, soundless laugh, and stepped past me again, settling himself at the kitchen table, one leg thrusting out from his chair.

He didn't look different at all, I realise, which should have surprised me perhaps, but the surprise was all in his arrival. I was too busy reading his *tone*, his mood, I think, to focus much on his appearance. It was always the mood you watched for with Freddy. People felt he was dangerous.

Here he was anyway, in my kitchen; barefoot, at ease and smiling to himself. Nine-tenths, at least, of the time we had spent together had been at a kitchen table — as I warmed the teapot, I was back again in my narrow house-by-the-swamp, twenty five years away across the straits of Hecate.

The first time, unannounced, he'd come visiting I knew nothing about him, yet I'd found myself wondering as he sat looking around, with one arm looped over his chair back, if what I sensed behind that compelling mask of a face was an incredulity — at himself, in this home; like a mountain bandit, lounging under safe-conduct in a residence, a tame fox scratching its ear in a henhouse. Mishka, my fey grey cat, jumped up on his knee as she did on each subsequent visit, and drowsed, while we talked, against the massive brown forearm with its faded jailcraft tattoo.

I looked now, as I had back then, for the con man at work. He seemed far less concerned with the impression he was making. And a quirk of amusement kept tightening his lips as though a private joke were unfolding.

I brought the tea things to the table and started to pour for us both. "Things going okay for you these days?"

"Oh I've been through the changes," he said, eyes darting to mine for a moment. "Changing back, changing forth . . . "

He turned his cup slowly around with his finger.

"I've got some travelling to do," he said, with that half-surfaced smile at his lips again. "Got some connections to make, some debts to pay off, before I head home.

"Got something for you here," he said.

He leaned back and eased something out of his pocket. It was one of those fine-woven spruce-root pokes that some of the old Haida ladies still make. There was a design painted on it, a wolf perhaps, I'm not sure: garish blue as though it had been done in felt marker. Typical Freddy, I thought, and at once he looked straight up at me, into that moment we had long ago learned to laugh at, once we had named it, early in every visit — the riccochet, the skate between his black Haida eyes and my Celtic blues. No escaping the challenge, whatever the good will.

And the little spruce-root sack wasn't for me. He pulled out a plastic bag from it, and some blue zigzag papers, and started crumbling a golden bud onto the table.

He hadn't touched his tea. I sipped mine and watched his fingers in silence as he constructed a joint with the squinting concentration he'd have given to a carving. "You laid some hash on me that time," he said, "that I didn't get round to paying you for."

"C'mon, Freddy," I said, "that must have been twenty years ago," and I laughed. "There's a statute of limitations, you know."

"No such thing," he said. "Not now. Never was."

"Well there is in my memory," I told him. I didn't want to smoke dope with Freddy; maybe I suspected a ploy to catch me off guard in some way.

He just held up the joint, a fat, humpbacked one, as if for my admiration. There was a book of matches beside a candle on the table. He lit the joint, took a quick triple-draw at it, and sat back while the smoke eddied down from his nostrils. His hand came towards me, proferring the smoke. "No, you go ahead," I said.

He leaned forward, took another deep draw, and held out the joint, daring me. Holding the smoke in, "Pelée," he said, or it sounded like "Pelée."

I thought of the killer volcano of Martinique, of the soccer star, of the weeping woman of Hawaii. I took the joint from his fingers. Maybe it was "Maui wowie", the legendary weed of the seventies.

But you never knew with Freddy: sometimes he'd say things you couldn't work out at all; you'd wonder if you'd heard him aright, if maybe he'd just said something in Haida that sounded like gnomic English. Once he turned to my daughter and said, "There's a hand inside your head," and she said, "I know," whether out of politeness or not, and he said, "Room for two," and then went back to talking about the comet Cahoutec and the girl he knew in Vancouver who'd taken her grandfather's spyglass up Grouse Mountain to get a closer look, and got lost for three weeks.

I didn't really know — I still don't — what troubles Freddy had been in back then; people just hinted at things, for some reason. There was blood on his hands, no doubt, but whose blood? It does make a difference. I handed the joint back. "I'll pass now," I said. "I've got work to do."

"We all got work to do." He stood up, and held out the joint till I had to take it. "Another night gone to pot," he said.

If I'd made that old joke, I'd have felt white and foolish. I never will fathom how that works. Just the fact of self-consciousness, maybe. Meanwhile I was left holding the joint while he strolled off through my living room.

He stood in front of the bookcase in the corner, staring at my things. Arosi, Ashante and Sepik — the particular treasures on the top shelf are part of the medley that is, I suppose, my mind; I can only guess what secrets and memories they share with each other from their times before me, what whispery pidgin or macaronic they've evolved in the corners I've housed them in, what the carved faces see . . .

But hanging on the wall above them is a necklace of eagle claws, the bird washed up on the sands below Tlell, the deerskin thongs and sachets sewed up by my friend Yvonne who shared that house-by-the-swamp with me then. A medley again: the thongs adorned with fragments of baltic amber, the pendant a bone harpoon point I had found near a long-dead village. And her patient work through the evenings at this love-gift for me, another power and memory.

Hung from the same nail, at the necklace's heart, is an argillite pendant, a sleeping raven, its beak tucked down upon its breast. Eagle and Raven, the great matrilineal clans of Haida Gwaii.

"Remember?" I said from the doorway. "The Sleeping Raven you gave me?" He didn't look round.

"You bought it," he said. "I sold it to you. Seventy-five bucks."

"I remember it as a gift," I said.

"I couldn't sleep that night," he said, and his hand went out towards the carving, but did not touch it. "I got up before light and went out on the beach, and I watched a raven asleep on a hemlock branch. I went back to the house and sat on the steps and started to carve him. And after the people got up, I went back down the shore, and sat on a log with the tide running in, and got him finished."

It's a tiny thing, about the size of a thumb-joint, the feathers a pattern of scallops, the feet hooked around an invisible branch. Only the eyes, somehow open and closed at once, belong in the formal traditions of Freddy's people.

I went over and stood beside him. Through the reefer's aroma he smelled of the islands: the moss and the rain and the salt-barbed currents of cedar smoke. We stood, with our separate memories and the small finger-brush intimacies that come with sharing a joint. But still I wondered, what did he really want?

He turned away. "Wish I had time to check out all the things I've made."

He crossed the room behind me and I whirled round, suspicious again, though of what I'm not sure. He sat down again, by the table; his casual way seemed to challenge me.

"Why no shoes?" I asked, as much as anything for something to say.

"My feet been in prison too long — look." He folded one leg across his knee, gripping the ankle in both hands to show me the sole. Unexpectedly slender, it was fissured with cracks and plateaus like an aerial photo. He flared and wriggled his toes, laughing at them. "Building some good calluses there," he said, putting his foot down again. "Like the Old People, eh?"

I wish I could remember more of what we talked about. What he talked about that is. I wish I'd payed more attention.

I can blame the drug partly, I guess. The way my thoughts began, and then slipped out of sight, like carousel horses which I hoped would come round again if I waited long enough.

But I was also too taken up with *watching* Freddy. His face was ancestral, that's the only way I can express it: like a portrait that after two hundred years still offers the living features of the dead. A face you might see, too, in an Edward Curtis photograph. And he was more interesting to watch — or so I assumed from past experience — than to listen to: for he'd always spoken essentially to himself, though he wanted response and approval, and the criminal optimism of his plans was depressing after a while.

Oh, he talked about finding "a better handle on life", I know that. And he was going home with things to accomplish. Which I'd heard before.

But he said a lot more than that, and the subject kept changing. He was excited, intent, and I was just listening in.

"I can't keep up with you," I told him at last. "You're way ahead of me."

He stopped, with that up-tilted chin that is part of the Haida language, a basic challenge, and I reached across the table to grab his hand, to say *Hey, no offence: I'm just drifting.* His eyes were suddenly dangerous: *Don't touch me* they said.

But then he laughed, as though the joke I'd been sensing throughout had at last broken through. He rubbed his hands along his thighs, "This is easy," he said. And looked up again, carefree and almost shy. "I gotta go."

It was so sudden. And I was totally relieved. I followed him to the door and held out my hand, expecting the centurion shake they'd all used in my time on the Queen Charlottes, but his palm merely glided across mine before he stepped outside.

I called out, "*Haaw'aa!*" thank you, the only Haida word from my tiny vocabulary that came to mind, as he jogged across my lawn into the box-elder shadows. I saw him jump onto the low retaining wall of my yard, up to street level, and he was gone.

I listened for a car, but heard nothing for five minutes before I went inside.

I was definitely stoned. I sat back down in my kitchen. He hadn't touched the tea I'd made him. I drank it for him; the drug was drying out my mouth.

I was reaching that state of lassitude where three, at least, of the Seven Sins become, if not friends exactly, no longer adversaries, when the phone rang on the wall just beside me.

I grabbed it without thinking, and at once regretted it. It had been a long time since I'd spoken on the phone under the influence, and if this wasn't a close friend I'd probably sound incoherent.

It was a woman whose first novel I was editing at the time, and I didn't yet know her well enough to discard my professional half-mask. But what was the point? My laboured efforts to concentrate and respond made me sound doleful, if not stupid. After two attempts to discuss structure and voice, I gave up.

"Look," I said, "this is a little hard to explain. Someone I haven't seen for years has just this minute left my house. He was here and gone so fast I can hardly believe he was here. He came in, sat down, smoked a joint and took off. But the point is, I'm completely roofed and I'm not going to make any sense tonight. I'll call you tomorrow, okay?"

She seemed merely amused. I hung up.

All I really wanted to do was turn off the lights, go and lie on my bed with the window wide open, and listen to the coyotes.

And doing that, I began to think about Freddy. It was easier to do now that he wasn't there in person, talking, insisting.

He was so potent, yet so lost.

Freddy could have been a wonderful carver if he'd worked on it. He'd get crazy, original notions and go at it like a fiend for a day or two till he was done. But then he'd slacken right off, for some reason or other: maybe he'd made enough cash, maybe people didn't respond to his work as he expected. And then he'd leave the islands.

A few generations back he might have been an innovator, a man with respect (or an outlaw like the legendary K'uundong'a). Who knows, given the Haida cosmology, he may have been all of those. But in this life anyway he relied upon inspiration, on being in the mood, or on the need to turn something out for quick money.

With the deadly escape hatch of heroin.

Yet I was exhilarated by his visit, and grateful. I loved the thought, as I replayed it in my mind, of an artist revisiting something he'd made years ago and remembering its making and the man he had been then himself. I could hug the fact that that had happened in my living room. The sleeping raven seemed a treasure twice over.

Sleep came towards me in the soft, soft darkness like an ecstasy. The coyotes were crying in the infinite distance as my bones rocked and settled in my flesh, drifting down into forgetfulness.

So I was late to wake, and moving pretty slowly.

It had rained in the night. Everywhere down the lane, as I walked to the post office, there were lilac petals: plastered to the wet earth, floating on the rain-filled wheel ruts. At one point I saw below me the roof of the United Church and the quick flock of waxwings that were even then whistling above my head.

> As by some puddle I did play
> Another world within it lay.

I love it when poetry surfaces to the occasion. My head was clearing already. Old Thomas Traherne, whose poems lay undiscovered for 200 years, and whose sense of Grace was the simplicity of childhood:

> That through a little watery chink
> Which one dry ox or horse might drink,
> We other worlds should see,
> Yet not admitted be . . .

Spring had come to stay: you could tell somehow, from the rain-washed air and the green creeping into the hills, there'd be no more killing frosts. I bounded up the post office steps, greeting other citizens, though I'd forgotten my keys and had to ask the postmistress to empty my mailbox. And I walked back down the lane in the sunlight.

One of the letters was from Susan, my oldest friend and adoptive sister, who also shared that house-by-the-swamp and writes marvellous letters. I opened it as I walked;

when the sun is out I can read without glasses. There was a nine of diamonds playing card and a poem, as well as the letter which I read as I weaved and splashed absent-mindedly through the puddles.

Most of it described the wake for our old friend Robin in Victoria the previous Saturday. It was wicked, ironic and heartfelt as her letters always are. Then, as I crossed over to my house: *When I arrived home after the 'service' there was a message on our machine from Henry in Masset . . .*

The words were for Stephen, her husband: an intimate, cryptic message between more-than-friends, and not mine to repeat, except for two lines: *Freddy Y. kicked the bucket. Died of an overdose in an alley.*

I walked down to my front door. Opened it, went inside, closed it and leaned back against it like a TV actor.

Fairy tales end with a token — the ring or the flower or fragrance left behind from the dream time. But I didn't examine the ashtray, or the cups unwashed in the sink. I looked at my empty room — at the table and chairs, the space of blank carpet before my bookshelf, the carved, watchful faces — and waited to be spelled out of memory, like the kids in *Rewards & Fairies*, as if the pages of Susan's letter were the oak, ash and thorn leaves which erase impossible things.

I was still holding her letter when I started to laugh.

I looked over at the raven, asleep in his wreath of eagle's claws, and I saw — as clearly as I saw the room where I stood — the beach at Masset, as the sun comes up across the wide inlet, and the carver who sits there making a bird into stone.

♈ ♈ ♈

ACKNOWLEDGEMENTS

Some of these stories, or versions of them, have previously appeared in the following collections:

"Deathbed", in *White Lies & Other Fictions* and *White Lies & Other Fictions + 2* (Exile Editions, Toronto).

"Maria", in *Wormwood* (Exile Editions).

"The Merchant", "The Glass Sphere" and "The Widow" in *Waking In Eden* (Exile Editions).

"Shan Val Mór" and "Brother Dael's New Year" in *Through The Eyes Of A Cat* (Sono Nis Press, Victoria).

The Introduction and "Guardians" appeared in *The Malahat Review*.

"Bolt" appeared in *Exile*.

A grant from the Saskatchewan Arts Board gave me time to finish this book, and I'm more than grateful for that.

The cover photograph, "Islanders of Innisheer", was taken in 1898 by J.M. Synge.

[A note on the story, "Maria": Young people like Terry think and feel through music. I wanted to show this. But though you can steal any song in the world off the internet and not pay the artist a cent, a writer who, for example, wants to use one line of a Joni Mitchell song is going to be charged $250, and it's the writer, not the publisher, who must pay it. You can resort to parody, or interpret as I have done. I really wish I could have used the words of Joni Mitchell, Chrissie Hynde and Van Morrison: they are a poetry that defines our time.]

NOTES ON "BROTHER DAEL'S NEW YEAR"

This story is set in the 1650s. The Mass was proscribed in Ireland and any Catholic cleric discovered was liable to execution or transportation to the Tobacco Isles (Bermuda). Many went into exile, some were hidden by the villagers, others retreated to islands like Inishboffin and took up hermits' lives, very like those practised from Skellig Micháel to Iceland (and possibly North America) seven or eight hundred years earlier.

The Wren's death: in some parts of Ireland 'the boys' still hunt the Wren on Boxing Day and parade him for tribute around the townland. Their song begins:

The Rann the Rann, the King of all Birds
Saint Stephen's Day was caught in the furze . . .

Throughout Europe the Robin Redbreast was the Wren's saturnalian adversary, and still appears on many Christmas cards, as well as in the nursery rhyme "Who Killed Cock Robin".

Bobbio was one of the most important Celtic (and hence eventually heretical) Christian monasteries in

Europe. It originally regarded Hy (Columcille's holy island of Iona) as its parent house. So did Kells. From these monasteries come two of the most beautiful illuminated Gospels of mediaeval times.

Europe was at this time still devastated by the effects and aftermath of the Thirty Years War.

The Pale, originally the Viking settlement round Dublin, was that area of Ireland controlled by the English and the essentially Protestant Anglo-Irish 'Ascendancy'. Cromwell's plan was to extend the Pale till it comprised the whole country except Connacht (which to him meant Clare and Galway).

Froichan mac Temnan was a wizard who threw a "druid's fence" round the army of the *Ard-Ri* (High King) Diormit Cerball, at the battle of Cul-drebne in 561. Columcille, who had caused the battle, won the day for the Ui-Neills by dispelling the magic mist. Then, racked with guilt at the immense slaughter, he went into exile.

Black Hugh O'Neill, a nephew of the great Owen Roe, was the only Irish military leader to make a fool out of Cromwell, (though some of the *tories*, outlaws, were very effective guerrillas). When Limerick at last fell, in 1651, O'Neill avoided execution on the grounds of his Spanish citizenship! Columcille, incidentally, was an O'Neill too.

Henry Ireton was Cromwell's general at Limerick. Though his behaviour did not rival that of Cromwell himself, still less the detestable Colonel Coote's, he was one of the most brutal implementers of the English policy against the Old Irish — *to Hell or to Connacht.* Cursed by the condemned Bishop Terence O'Brien, Ireton died three weeks after Limerick, of the Plague.